"Sand flies, lizards on the beach . . . Michael, help me!" Cathy begged. "Do something!"

He looked down at her, his eyes dark with amusement, half Boy Scout, half devil. "What would you like me to do?"

"Save me!"

"Okay." Without another word he picked her up and tossed her over his shoulder as he strode off up the beach. Silenced by sheer surprise, Cathy grabbed the waist of his shorts and held on tight. Finally, after he carried her to a shaded grove, he knelt and put her down on the sand.

"Better?" he asked.

She thought about it for a second. She was dizzy, her ears hummed, and he was awfully close. So close she could smell the saltwater and the sweat on him. "I'm not sure—"

"Maybe I'd better check your pulse," he whispered, and pressed his lips to the hollow of her throat. She closed her eyes as his delicious kisses warmed her everywhere. Then they stopped, and she opened her eyes.

Michael was staring down at her, his eyes hot and hungry, blue as the center of a flame. No man had ever looked at her like that before. If she said yes, it would burn her to ashes and she'd blow away on the wind. . . .

WHAT ARE *LOVESWEPT* ROMANCES?

They are stories of true romance and touching emotion. We believe those two very important ingredients are constants in our highly sensual and very believable stories in the *LOVESWEPT* line. Our goal is to give you, the reader, stories of consistently high quality that may sometimes make you laugh, sometimes make you cry, but are always fresh and creative and contain many delightful surprises within their pages.

Most romance fans read an enormous number of books. Those they truly love, they keep. Others may be traded with friends and soon forgotten. We hope that each *LOVESWEPT* romance will be a treasure—a "keeper." We will always try to publish

LOVE STORIES YOU'LL NEVER FORGET
BY AUTHORS YOU'LL ALWAYS REMEMBER

The Editors

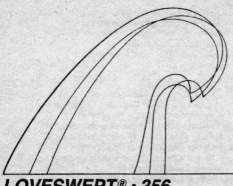

LOVESWEPT® · 356

Adrienne Staff and Sally Goldenbaum
The Great American Bachelor

 BANTAM BOOKS
NEW YORK · TORONTO · LONDON · SYDNEY · AUCKLAND

To our family and friends—
as always,
with love!
Adrienne and Sally

THE GREAT AMERICAN BACHELOR

A Bantam Book / October 1989

LOVESWEPT® *and the wave device are registered
trademarks of Bantam Books, a division of
Bantam Doubleday Dell Publishing Group, Inc.
Registered in U.S. Patent
and Trademark Office and elsewhere.*

*If you would be interested in receiving protective vinyl
covers for your Loveswept books, please write to this address
for information:*

*Loveswept
Bantam Books
P.O. Box 985
Hicksville, NY 11802*

ISBN 0-553-22026-8

Published simultaneously in the United States and Canada

*Bantam Books are published by Bantam Books, a division
of Bantam Doubleday Dell Publishing Group, Inc. Its trademark, consisting of the words "Bantam Books" and the
portrayal of a rooster, is Registered in U.S. Patent and
Trademark Office and in other countries. Marca Registrada.
Bantam Books, 666 Fifth Avenue, New York, New York 10103.*

PRINTED IN THE UNITED STATES OF AMERICA

O   0 9 8 7 6 5 4 3 2 1

One

Michael Winters stood with one hip resting against the bar, a scotch waiting near his hand. Across the room the dining area was filled with casually dressed diners. But here at the bar he was alone. He was glad for the solitude, glad to be watching instead of watched for a change. These few stolen minutes of privacy were more valuable than hard currency. All this recent publicity was grating, and he had had enough media attention to last him a long time. But after tonight it would be over. Or at least would be eased. Tomorrow he would get back to business, making decisions, issuing orders. So he stood there, grateful for the respite, letting his eyes roam the room, distanced, alone. He was not curious, or even interested in the people around him, just silent and watching. Then the attractive girl he had noticed earlier smiled.

Damn! he thought. There was a smile to knock

your legs out from under you! He tossed down a mouthful of scotch and stared at her. She was pretty but not stunning. Slim, more coltish than willowy. Nice legs. Lovely shoulders. Age? He took another sip and let it burn its way down his throat. Maybe mid-twenties. But there was something else. What? *Something.* Narrowing his dark eyes, he studied her with an expert gaze. What was it?

Cathy Stephenson felt the hairs lifting along her arms. The air-conditioning, she wondered. She hadn't noticed it before. Maybe this boring date was beginning to affect her physically. With a little shrug she glanced around the room. Stopped. Glanced back to the bar. A little click happened in her head. She knew that man . . . but how? She frowned, drawing her brows down over her wide brown eyes. She had caught him watching her and for a second had the oddest feeling that she knew him, recognized him. But no. A man like that she would not forget. And yet . . .

He put down his drink and met her eyes. Click.

Thump. Her heart made a strange noise. She took a quick look at Rod, her awful blind date, to see if he had heard it. But, typical of the evening, her date did not notice anything but himself. He continued to babble at her while tossing down drinks. She smiled reassuringly at him, nodded, then she looked back at the bar and the blood raced to her cheeks. The man had caught her staring.

Quickly she turned her attention back across the table to Rod. But all the little nerve endings at the nape of her neck were sending SOS's a mile a minute. Goodness, who was that, she wondered.

"Hey, doll, aren't ya'll impressed?" Rod demanded. "Tonight I wanted to bring you over here to the beach, give ya a sample of some real Florida cookin'. But I'll show you around Orlando sometime. Bet it's nothin' like Iowa—"

"Indiana," she corrected him. "I'm from Bloomington, Indiana."

"Well, I bet Indiana hasn't got anything to compare with Orlando. I mean, this town's booming! And have we got places to have fun: Church Street Station and Rosie O'Grady's, and some great bars down on South Orange Blossom Trail. I can even show you places that were here before all the tourists and you Yankees came bargin' in. Hey, don't feel bad. Not everyone can have life's advantages like me."

Cathy nodded and pasted a smile on her mouth.

"Native, that's me! You'll be glad you moved on down. As long as you don't let them work you to death at Tower Publishing; I mean, that sister of mine is one tough boss!"

Which was how Cathy had ended up here in the first place.

A blind date! Cathy had not been on one in years. But it was hard to say no when the VP who had just hired her as an assistant editor said she had a charming brother. Hard to say no when she suggested they double-date. Hard to say no when she called the night before with the flu, but said Rod was really looking forward to it.

For Cathy, under those circumstances, no was impossible.

So here she was, sitting in a crowded restaurant

in Florida. She should have been excited, she knew, since this was her first night out since she moved south; instead, she was annoyed and uncomfortable, having doubts not just about tonight, but about her boss, her new job, her whole move south. What if her boss was anything like Rod?

Rod rambled on again, and Cathy nodded in reply at the appropriate moments. She had the feeling he was happier with an audience—a captive audience—than he would have been if she actually tried to say something.

So she nibbled on oyster crackers, sipped a glass of white wine, prayed for the evening to come to a quick conclusion, shyly keeping her eyes away from the bar.

Shyness was not a problem for the man at the bar. Not shyness, or reticence, or timidity. No. He had always believed you nail your colors to the mast and you fight to keep them there! Of course, for the magazine interview he had said something far more subtle and sophisticated. But the truth was the same. And he was bold as brass. So he stared at the girl. What the hell was she doing with that loser, he wondered as he nursed his scotch in silence.

At the table Rod was getting louder and more obnoxious by the moment. "Try some 'gator tail!" he ordered. "Try the turtle soup. And loosen up. Relax." When he ordered his third drink, Cathy finally objected.

"Rod, two's enough. We have that long drive back to Orlando—"

"No problem. I'm not even feeling them."

"That's what worries me. How about if I drive back?" This was it. She would never accept a blind date again, not even for a boss.

"I said I'm fine. Lighten up."

"I don't want to lighten up. I either want to drive home or I want you to stop drinking."

"Hey, I—" Then he bit off his words and grinned at her, lacing his fingers behind his head. "Sure, you drive. Fine with me. I always wanted a chauffeur."

Dinner arrived at that moment. Cathy entertained a fleeting wish that he'd choke on his 'gator, but she pushed it away, determined to finish the evening on a positive note. She nibbled on her salad, carefully avoided looking at her entree, and strained for a glimpse of the ocean outside the windows.

That had been something, that first glimpse of the ocean! When she had stepped from the car, all she could see was ocean. It was dark as slate, and the rising moon had poured light over its surface like spilt milk. Or molten silver. Or a moth's pale, phosphorescent wing. Oh, and how it changed! Each second it was new, different, as the water heaved and rose and curled and crashed down on itself in spray and glory. Truly, that was something to write about someday, when she could do what she really wanted to do! She smiled, imagining it.

The man at the bar followed her gaze, wondering what she was thinking. What had made her smile like that? It couldn't have been her date.

"Off in dreamland again?" Rod smirked. He polished off his last drink and paid the check. Then he headed toward the door, not bothering to pull her chair out or hand her her sweater.

She followed, hesitating just once on the way to the door, almost unwillingly, near the bar. She glanced at the man. He was watching her, just as she knew he would be, with those intense blue, somehow familiar eyes, and an insane little smile leapt to her lips before she could bite it back. Get hold of yourself! she swore silently. Then she hurried, blushing, onto the porch.

The ocean was gone. A fat, thick fog had rolled in and all that was left of the Atlantic was its deep, disembodied roar. This evening was turning out to be a flop on all counts. With a sigh and a shrug she turned to Rod.

"Okay," she said, determined to carry this off with style. "How about the keys?"

He just looked at her.

"Rod," she said, trying to joke, "go ahead, toss me the keys. Here"—she was scooting backward, hands out like a receiver waiting for the football—"watch this catch! Come on, I'm ready."

"Forget it. I don't need you to drive me home." His voice was surly.

Anger made her gasp. She dug her heels in. "Rod, you said I could drive—"

"Now I'm saying you can't."

"But—"

"I'm fine, I told you. I had three little drinks. Hell, you want me to walk a straight line? Touch my finger to my nose?" He demonstrated as he spoke, every move and gesture dripping with sarcasm. "Want me to count backward from one hundred? Ninety-nine, ninety-eight, ninety-six, ninety—"

"Seven," she snapped, eyes flashing.

"That's what I said."

"Forget it. I'll get a ride."

"From Cocoa Beach to Orlando? At night? Who you gonna ask, huh, some guy inside?"

"That's not your problem," she called over her shoulder. "I'll call a cab."

"Sure. That should cost only about a hundred bucks, hundred and fifty—"

She tossed her head, eyes pricking with tears of frustration. "I don't care."

She heard the pounding of his footsteps, then felt his hand on her shoulder. "Okay, fine. Here're the keys. I don't want you telling some sob story to my sister. Shoot . . ." he drawled, "you certainly know how to kill an evening."

Cathy took the keys and marched to the car without looking back. She didn't care if he came along or not!

She did not see the man watching from the doorway.

That's better, he thought as he stepped outside and leaned back against the door, arms crossed loosely over his broad chest. He had followed them out, poised to rescue her if she needed help. Not that he wanted to get mixed up in anything. Hell, the magazine would just love that! Talk about poised and ready—there they were out there, not three hundred yards away on the company yacht.

He squinted into the fog. It was time to be getting back. He stretched his broad shoulders beneath the heavy cotton of his shirt. And he strode down toward the dock and the fourteen-foot Boston Whaler he had left tied up there. Tonight's party would be starting soon. And he had promised a few more pictures, a few more answers to a few more questions. All of this seemed trivial to him, but somehow most of his quotes became headlines.

A short distance away Cathy waited for Rod to climb into the passenger seat. "Buckle up," she ordered. He ignored her.

They pulled onto A1A, heading slowly north through the fog toward the turn that would lead back onto the highway and to Orlando. Cathy was nervous, and Rod was not helping.

"Move it, will ya? You've gone all of twenty yards. At this speed we'll get home next Tuesday!"

From behind, a car honked and Cathy jumped.

"Hey, get back in the right lane," Rod barked, reaching for the wheel.

She slapped his hand away. "I thought it was a left turn—"

"I'm taking you a different way. Here, I'll get the map. . . ." He flicked on the inside light. "See, ya go up to the end of the block. Slow down. Right here . . . no, next one . . . no wait, not here . . . give it a little speed, will ya!"

He pulled on the wheel and stepped on the gas, trapping her foot between his and the pedal as the car leapt forward, out of control.

"Let me drive!" she yelled, struggling to push him off her.

"Here's the bridge! I remember—" he muttered drunkenly.

"Rod, no!"

He spun the wheel hard to the right and left the lights and traffic of A1A behind them. The car bumped and bucked down a dirt road she could not even see, but she could hear the gravel kick up around them. He was leaning across her, hanging on to the wheel, blinded by the light inside and the total darkness outside. And she was shoved down against the door, arms crossed in front of her face, begging, "Stop, please stop, oh—"

Suddenly the car jumped a step up onto something wooden. There was the rat-a-tat-tat of wheels racing along wooden planks and then flashes of movement, and the startled faces of fishermen, like photographs, flipped by the moving windows of the car.

"Watch out for the people!" Cathy screamed, fighting for the steering wheel.

"People?"

"Oh, God—!"

The fishermen leapt back out of the way and watched in stunned surprise as the car, still doing forty, neared the end of the pier, smashed the rail into splinters, and sailed through the air, hanging motionless for a moment before it dove straight down into the black, indifferent ocean.

Two

Shouts. The rumble of a car. The high, tremulous wail of Cathy's scream.

Michael heard all three through the muffling blanket of the fog. Gunning the outboard, he raced the Boston Whaler through the murky blackness toward the noise.

"Move, move!" he urged the little boat, but soon he had to cut the engine to idle, afraid of getting too close, afraid of running right into them. Into her. He knew it was her: the brown-haired, smiling girl from the restaurant. It was almost as if he had been waiting, listening to know she was safe, waiting and listening for the first sign of trouble if she were not. Every muscle in his body was tense. He peered through the fog, scanning the rolling gray surface of the water. Straining, he leaned over the side of the boat, listening for a shout, a cry. He took shallow breaths, fighting the adrenaline that flooded through his muscles. "Come on, come on," he said under his breath, "I'll find you."

Suddenly off to his left he heard a commotion and shouting, and then the fishing pier floated into sight. A crowd had gathered at its end, and he saw a wet, suddenly sober young man half climbing, half lifted out of the water. "We've got the driver! We've got him!" came a disembodied shout.

About to turn the little boat back out toward open water and gun the throttle, Michael stopped. *Him?* He cast about slowly, again peering through the fog. "Come on . . ." And then he spotted the girl. She was gasping and struggling, barely keeping her head above water.

Michael cut the engine, stood up, and dove in. He sliced through the waves, his arms pulling against the current, straining for a glimpse of that dark head. Come on. Come on . . . Gulping a chestful of air, he dove under, eyes burning with the sting of salt, the tide yanking the loafers right off his feet. It seemed an eternity before he found her. Limp, half conscious, she was being tossed about by the undertow like a little rag doll. Three powerful strokes and he had an arm around her and was aiming for the surface, for air.

They came up choking, fighting for air, saltwater streaming into their eyes and mouths. "It's okay. I've got you," he sputtered, but Cathy was totally panicked, gulping air and water together, crying, batting wildly at him, at the water. She didn't feel his arms or hear his voice. He held her tight against him, but she was slippery as a fish, and all her struggles pulled them down under the whitecaps.

"Damn!" he swore. "Take it easy; you'll drown both of us! Easy, easy . . ." Kicking hard to stay afloat, he tucked her under one arm and freed the other for swimming. Still fighting, she gave him a good hard kick in the shin. He yelped. "Now, where's the damn boat?" His eyes combed the waves; the little Boston Whaler was bobbing crest to crest just a few yards away. "Okay, darlin', here we go."

He pulled her through the water, the muscles in his legs, thighs, and arms burning in protest. Then his fingers closed over the wooden side of the little boat, and he pulled it closer, took a searing breath, and tossed her up into it. For one second he leaned his forehead against the side, lights dancing behind his eyelids, his lungs aflame. Then he pulled himself up and over.

She lay still, eyes closed, breathing weakly, a mermaid flung onto the dry wooden deck.

Crouching down, he checked her breathing, her color. He brushed the wet hair from her face. With the touch came a strange, unexpected feeling, a rush of tenderness that made him want to protect her against all dangers, battle dragons, tilt at windmills . . . at the very least, kiss the saltwater off her pale lips. But, as always, the practical won out over the romantic in Michael Winters.

He cushioned her head on a pillow made from his wet clothes, and then steered swiftly and expertly out to the yacht for help.

Cathy dreamed she was in her grandmother's house back in Indiana, wrapped in the warm, plump arms of the wonderful woman who always smelled like berries and wild corn.

Gap was rocking her slowly, rhythmically, in the large oak rocker next to the fireplace in her living room.

The motions were wonderful and comforting, except Gap had forgotten to light the fire, and Cathy was so terribly cold that her body ached. But Gap knew that, and she held her close, murmuring that she'd be all right.

Cathy smiled and pressed closer. "G'night, Gap—"

"Nightcap?" The voice was deep and laced with a relieved sort of laughter. "She wants a nightcap. Harry, grab that brandy decanter."

Cathy paused in her dream. Gap's voice should be light and melodious, not deep and rumbling.

"You're going to be all right," the voice continued, and when Cathy pressed her head into Gap's chest, it was hard and strong . . . and flat. She forced open her heavy eyelids.

"What . . . ?" The small word was spoken against warm, damp skin that smelled vaguely of open air and saltwater and aftershave.

"It's okay." The man's dark head bent down until his forehead almost touched hers. "You sure scared the hell out of us."

Voices in the background murmured, but all Cathy could see were the dark blue eyes that matched the deepest part of the ocean. He was holding her, and she seemed to be wrapped in a towel or blanket. She was freezing. And wet. At a loss for an alternative, Cathy smiled weakly. "Hello."

"Hello yourself."

"I'm soaking wet."

The stranger smiled. "That you are, mermaid.

Swimming at night, and fully dressed, is not a good idea. One does get wet."

Cathy moved one hand up to her chest. Her hands spread out beneath the blanket until she could feel her dress. It was still there, thank heaven, but when she wiggled her feet, she knew her shoes were gone. Her new sandals. Frowning, she gave a small sigh of dismay. And then it all came back in a flash: the gator tail. Her date. And the car flying off the end of the dock.

Her hand flew to her mouth. "Oh, my God!"

Michael looked up at the others. His smile broadened. "She remembers. She'll be fine."

Cathy turned her head and looked around. Through the haze she could see that she was in a small, richly decorated room with round windows and low furniture. It smelled of polished wood and the sea. That was all her mind and senses could sort out. The lights were dim and the muscular arms of the man holding her prevented her from seeing much more, but she knew there were people around, more strangers.

Michael, who had not taken his eyes off the lovely sea nymph's face for more than a second, saw the flash of fear in her eyes. He turned to the other people in the room. "Someone order some soup. I'll take care of the rest. You can get back to the party."

There were voices and shuffling feet, doors opening and closing, but Cathy was numb to it all. Her head was filled with a collage of action: the car flying through the air, the jolting impact of hitting the water, and then the slow, sinking sensation as water poured into the car as it went down. She remembered Rod screaming just before they hit water, and she remembered the feel of him leaving the driver's seat almost immediately, his legs kicking madly as he pushed himself through the window. And she had followed frantically, blindly, trying to swim but too scared, too tired.

"I was drowning . . ." She shivered, hearing the words and knowing how true they were.

"You're all right now," he assured her.

"Am I? Am I really?" She trembled, remembering the panic, the darkness, the water in her eyes and mouth and throat.

"Yes." His voice was low but commanding. He tipped her chin up so she had to meet his eyes. "You're safe and you're fine. Trust me."

"All right," she whispered, and snuggled against him. And then she suddenly realized that she was cradled in some man's arms. She tried to push herself away from him, but the movement sent sharp spears of pain through her head.

"Hey, it's okay. Take it easy. You swallowed a bit of the ocean before I got to you. You must feel like hell."

Her fingers found their way to her head and she rubbed it gently. "It hasn't been one of my better nights," she admitted.

They were on a small couch, and Cathy inched herself over slowly until she was no longer so close to him. The room was cold and she shivered, pulling the blanket tight. The man kept his arm at her back, supporting her, and she found the strength of his body next to hers undeniably comforting.

"How did you get yourself into such a mess?" he asked.

"I was on a blind date."

His laughter was rich and genuine, rising from deep down in his chest, filling the shadowy room, bringing warmth to her wet bones.

She smiled and ducked her head. "I know it's crazy. And the truth is, I *never* get into situations like that. Honest!"

Afraid she was babbling, she bit her lip and stared down at her lap. The numbing fear had nearly subsided, replaced by an awkward awareness of how she must look, soaking wet, a transparent sundress clinging to her breasts beneath this stranger's plaid blanket. Maybe if she knew his name she'd feel more at ease. "I'm Cathy," she said firmly. "Cathy Stephenson." She held out her hand.

Michael closed it in his. "How do you do. I'm Michael Winters." Her hand was still cold from her plunge into the ocean, and he rubbed it lightly, watching the bluish color turn pink beneath his fingers.

Cathy's eyelids fluttered closed. The heat that began in her hand, where he touched her, spread smoothly and quickly up her arm and through her body. She shook her head slightly and forced herself to focus on her situation. "The car . . . Rod . . . is he all right?"

"Fine," Michael said shortly. But seeing the worry in her wide brown eyes, he touched her cheek reassuringly. "He's probably sitting in a shore bar right now, drying off, telling his story to a rapt if somewhat drunken audience. And I wouldn't bet on him mentioning you. Except for his drowned TransAm, the bum'll be fine."

Tears gathered on Cathy's lashes. "Oh, he is a bum! But what if . . . what if you hadn't been there? What if you weren't there to save me . . . ?" Her chin trembled, and the tears spilled down her cheeks.

Michael brushed them away with his strong fingers. "But I was. And you're fine," he insisted. "No sense scaring yourself now." His eyes were gentler than his voice, so Cathy looked deep into them to find her courage.

"You're right." She nodded quickly.

"Of course I'm right." He hid the unexpected discomfort he felt under those tears and that trusting gaze.

Cathy gave a little smile. His arm had not moved; it was tight on her back, a warm brace holding her shivering body. She licked her lips and gave a little shrug. "I don't know quite the right thing to say here. I've never had to do this before."

"What's that?" Michael brushed a stray wet curl from her face.

"Thank someone for saving my life."

"You haven't?" One dark brow lifted straight up in mock surprise.

"No," she answered, knowing she was being teased and liking him for it. "This is my first time."

"I can see you've led a sheltered life," he replied smoothly.

She laughed. "True. Until tonight!" And picturing the letter she'd write home to Indiana, she had to laugh out loud again. Gap had told her to go have an adventure, but surely she could not have meant this! Then, worried that Michael was going to think she was crazy, she stole a glance his way. He was still watching her with that calm, steady look.

"Relax. It's all over now," he said.

Cathy nodded. "I know. But even if this is all some strange sort of dream and I wake up tomorrow in my brand-new apartment and find out I've imagined this whole thing, I *still* want to thank you before it ends."

Michael watched her as she spoke. Her eyes seemed to reflect the lifts in her voice, lighting up then widening as she became animated. She was enchanting, a curly-haired mermaid without a pretentious bone in her lovely body.

"Then before it ends," he answered softly, surprising himself, "let me offer to drop into a few more of your dreams and rescue you from quicksand . . . swamps . . . you name it."

Cathy laughed, startled by his intensity. "Then you think it's a dream too?"

"I don't know, Cathy. I do know that in real life I don't often have this much unexpected pleasure."

Cathy blushed. This gorgeous dark-haired stranger looked like he wouldn't have anything *but* pleasure in his life. Yachts? Of course. And beautiful women and fast cars and private jets and . . .

"Why, you're the man from the restaurant! The one at the bar!"

"I thought you realized that—" he began, but she cut him short.

"So you saw everything! All night! I mean, you were like my guardian angel, watching over me!"

"I wouldn't put it quite like that." Michael grinned. "I just couldn't help watching a beautiful woman."

"Me?" She laughed, waving away the compliment. But she leaned forward, eyeing him carefully, studying him intently.

He frowned. "What are you doing?"

"Now, this *is* crazy. Maybe my brain's just waterlogged, but I *know* I know you. I thought so even in the bar. I know I've seen you, heard your name—"

She stopped, head tipped to one side. And then she grinned and tapped his chest with one finger. "I know! I *do* know you. You're Michael Winters!"

"I just told you that." He laughed. But his eyes were narrowed, his body tense.

"Yes, but you're Michael Bradford Winters. *The* Michael Winters. You were just on the cover of *Time*: The Great American Bachelor! Oh my!"

"Oh my what?" he asked, leaning back so that a great space opened up between them, eighteen inches that felt like eighty. His arm rested along the sofa back. One leg was crossed over the other. He was the perfect image of elegant nonchalance.

"Oh my goodness," she answered softly, dismayed by this sudden coldness. "That's all I meant. Did I say something wrong?"

"Nothing." But he seemed to be waiting.

Cathy shrugged. "Nice place you've got here," she offered gamely.

His mouth twitched into a smile. "It's not mine, it's the publisher's. The company yacht. This stateroom was empty, so we brought you here." His eyes searched her wide brown eyes, watching for something he didn't find there, coyness or calculation.

Unexpectedly he smiled. "I told them to bring you something to eat. Something warm. Is soup all right?"

"Fine," she murmured, feeling flustered. "I . . . I don't want to put you to a lot of trouble. Really, don't bother. I can—"

Michael's grin cut through her objections. "You can what? Swim back to the restaurant? Call a cab?" he asked, teasing her until she smiled again.

"I guess not."

"Do you live near the beach?"

Cathy's hand flew to her mouth. "No, no, I don't. *Nowhere* near. I live in Orlando."

"Hmmm. Now, that's an interesting problem. It's quite a hike to Orlando."

Cathy straightened up. It might be a problem, but it was *her* problem, and she was not going to drop one more ounce of trouble in this man's lap. "Nope, no problem. I'll rent a car."

"Cash or credit card?" His grin flashed wickedly.

Cathy groaned. Cash, credit card, driver's license— everything was in her purse at the bottom of the ocean! "Now what am I going to do?" She bit down hard on her lower lip and pulled the blanket back around her.

"No problem." The irrational urge to protect her overwhelmed him again. "I'll take care of everything. Later. It's no bother."

Cathy thought about that for a minute. She already owed this man her life. Adding a few more hours and a rental car were mere drops in the bucket. "All right. That would be nice, Michael." She offered him a half smile. "Thank you. I don't know how I'll ever repay you."

An interesting thought crossed Michael's mind, but he pushed it away, biting back the sensual smile that had climbed to his lips. Instead, he drew a deep breath, crossed both hands behind his dark head, and narrowed his eyes. "You don't owe me a thing; it's my pleasure."

While they talked, a steward left a silver tray with something hot and aromatic on the table near the windows. Michael glanced at it. "Looks like soup's on, Cathy. How about having a bite to eat while we talk about what to do next?"

"If you don't mind, I'd love a hot shower first, and something dry to put on." She looked hopefully around the room, willing something to appear.

"No problem. I'll get you my robe. I'll be right back, okay?"

"Great. Thanks." She pulled the blanket tight around a new layer of goose bumps. The minute he left she scurried into the bathroom and only reached an arm out when he knocked. "Thanks. Out in a minute!" she called, and locked the door.

While she showered, Michael poured two glasses of wine.

When the magazine had arranged this weekend celebration, he had felt compelled to accept, squeezing it into an already painfully overloaded agenda. And, he had to admit, he had wanted a first-hand look at this ship. *La Cygne*, the swan, as she was so aptly named, was a one-hundred-and-thirty-foot oceangoing yacht with a steel hull and a cruising speed of 12.5 knots. And inside it was as elegant as the Plaza, the food as wonderful, the service as fine. There was even a rosewood baccarat table from Monaco and a hot tub large enough to hold twenty people with room left over to wiggle toes, or whatever else there was to wiggle. And the publisher had agreed to route the trip so it included his business appointment tomorrow morning in the Abacos.

But Michael had been bored. He had been bored often lately, in the midst of multimillion-dollar real estate deals and acquisitions, and it worried him because he considered it an ungracious state of mind . . . and a weakness.

Cathy's appearance had changed all that, at least for a few hours. This girl, with her wide brown eyes and curly brown hair, her lovely long legs and her beautiful skin, made him feel unexpectedly, crazily, like the boy next door. Young. Hopeful. Expecting great things to happen in a great and wonderful world. He had felt like that once, years earlier, before he had gotten everything he wanted and found out it wasn't enough. But this girl, she still had dreams behind her dark eyes. She had a smile that knocked a man over, it was so filled with joy and spontaneity. Give me a little of that, he thought, taking a sip of the wine. Give me a taste of that again.

He placed his glass back next to hers on the table. Who knew, maybe Cathy Stephenson would provide enough fuel for him to get through the next couple of days? And there was no doubt in his mind that he would enjoy repaying that debt.

"Hi," Cathy said from the doorway.

Michael looked up. She was standing still, her slender shape almost lost in his terry robe. The light from the bathroom behind her cast a shimmering glow around her head, and her face was flushed from the heat of the shower. Her lips were parted, her eyes shining. A bead of water dripped off her cheek onto the rise of her breasts and disappeared.

Michael felt a surge of desire rise in his groin, and his imagination raced through the familiar moves that would end in a moment of passion. Guaranteed. A word, a look, a touch . . . all combined with who he was, what he owned, what he controlled. It always worked. But he knew he would not use it tonight, not with her.

Instead, he cocked his dark head to one side and studied her, the delicate features of her face revealing the vulnerability that played like some inner light across those gently sculpted bones. The softness, the openness in her expression, caught him off guard. He found himself in the impossible position of still wanting, on the one hand, to sweep her up in a passionate embrace and carry her off to bed . . . and, on the other, to offer her a glass of warm milk.

Cathy tipped the scales. "Umm, something sure does smell good."

"Hungry?" Michael managed to ask around the tightness in his throat.

"Well, I tried, but I really couldn't eat much in that restaurant."

"I noticed."

She smiled, padded across the floor, and sat down at the table. "Please eat with me. I hate to eat alone."

"Do you eat alone often?" Michael pulled out the chair across from her and sat down.

"Never! I've always had family or roommates before. Before now, that is." She stirred her soup absentmindedly.

"And now?" Michael prompted her.

"Well, now I've moved into my own apartment in a strange city, so yes, I'll probably be eating alone a great deal." Cathy paused, holding her soup spoon in midair, considering her new life. "But I won't like it, I know that. I'll have to find some soup-eating buddy. Or get a cat."

"And before this? Where did you move from?"

"Bloomington, Indiana. A small town nearby, really. I grew up there. My grandmother, I call her Gap—"

"Gap?" He had heard it wrong then, earlier. The realization of what she had really said tugged his mouth up at the corners.

Color flooded her cheeks. "It's . . . it's an endearment," Cathy explained. "Anyway, Gap raised me after my folks died. We lived on a farm until I went to college, and then we moved into town with my aunt Tisha. After that, once I was working at the University Press and could afford the rent, I shared an apartment with some friends. So there was always someone to cook soup for, and share soup with. . . ." She pressed her lips closed, letting her eyes alone smile at him. "I *do* tend to talk a lot. Sorry."

"No, I'm really interested," he insisted, leaning back in his chair, his gaze steady and intense. "Then what?"

"Then I read about this opening at Tower Publishing in Orlando. I interviewed. They hired me. And now I'm the proud leasee of a brand-new apartment with lots of flowers and walls thin as tissue paper."

"And you're an editor?"

"Assistant editor, bottom rung." She frowned and plunked both elbows on the table and rested her chin on her hands. "To tell the truth, at the moment I don't know what to do about that. You see, 'the bum' was my new boss's brother. Small complication."

"Untenable situation. Find another job."

"Just like that?" She laughed, her brows zooming into her bangs.

"Just like that. You wouldn't want to work for that person. And you can do better than that job."

"And you can read my fortune? What do you have, a crystal ball?"

"Better than that. A lot of experience. And enough connections to make things happen. Is it an editorial job you want?"

Her shoulders were shaking with silent laughter, her eyes sparkling. "That easy, huh? Well, then I want"—she tipped her head, studying the ceiling, or beyond—"I want a cabin in the woods, and a huge old desk to write at, or an apartment in the middle of some big, bustling city, and lots of people to meet and discuss books with, and a huge old desk to write at, or—"

"Or both?" he finished for her, his gaze touching lightly on her cheekbones, her chin, her smiling mouth, thinking how easy it was for him to get those things: a cabin, an apartment. Anything. Anywhere. "And is that what you really want to do? Write?"

"Yes," she answered honestly, meeting his eyes.

"That is what I really want to do. And I will. Some-day. For now there are bills to pay, and money to send home, and I'll get myself a good, practical edi-torial job at another company."

"Let me help you."

Teasing, she tossed her head. "And what makes you think I need help? They may be knocking down my door the minute I get back to Orlando."

"They will if they've got any sense at all."

"Thank you." Her smile was warm, a flame, a sunburst. "And thanks for the offer. But I'm sure I'll be fine. And right now I'm happy to be alive and sharing soup with you."

And that was the truth, Cathy realized with sur-prise. Foolish but true. She made a habit of study-ing people, and she knew well that Michael Winters was from another world, another planet, for all the differences between them. But for the moment, in this absolutely absurd situation she had fallen into, he was a wonderful mealmate, no matter who he might be in real life.

She swallowed a spoonful of soup then. "Chowder! I really shouldn't eat something I've just been swim-ming with." She laughed, and took a long drink of wine. "I suppose I ought to watch this." She nodded toward the wine. "I wouldn't want to sleep away my few hours on this floating palace. Perhaps I could use some of it for a story. Throw in a few outrageous lies. Sell it to some lurid tabloid!"

She took another gulp of wine.

What the shower had begun the wine was finishing —a lovely loosening of her body. After the terrible tenseness of this day, it was certainly what the doc-tor ordered.

Michael watched her face and body relax, and with the gentle easing of her muscles, the robe slipped down her shoulders and a teasing V of silken flesh appeared. Her skin looked rich as honey, and for a moment Michael wondered if she would taste honey-sweet if he were to lean over and touch his lips to her skin right there.

Whoa! Michael pushed his chair back from the table roughly and stood up.

Cathy was startled. "Is everything okay?"

"Just fine." There was an undisguised edge of irritation to his voice.

"Funny, you don't look so fine." Cathy followed his lead and stood quickly. The movement was foolish. The blood from her head drained as quickly as she had drained her wineglass, and she grabbed for the edge of the table.

Michael was at her side in an instant. "Cathy, sit!" But he didn't allow her to sit. Instead, he scooped her up as he had wanted to do all evening, and he pressed her clean, lovely body into his chest. "It'll be okay," he murmured into the soft curls of her hair.

He carried her back to the couch and sat down, drawing her gently onto his lap. "It was too much, that's all. The wine and the day had a bit of a rift."

Cathy closed her eyes and let her head drop against his chest. Rift, shmift, she thought drowsily. This was what she needed, this gorgeous man holding her close. She tilted her head back. "Am I going to spend the rest of my life drowning or fainting so you can pick up the pieces?"

Michael touched her cheek. "It has definite possibilities."

"I'm not usually like this, you know."

"So you say," he joked, his voice gone low and husky with desire. But it was not just the pressure of her warm, lovely body wedged into his lap, it was the sweet smell of her skin and the brush of her soft hair against his cheek.

"Cathy," he said finally, "I'm either going to put you down right now, and cover you up until you're feeling clear-headed enough to dress, or I'm going to kiss you."

"That's a tough one," she whispered, looking straight into his eyes. But when she tilted her head back and tipped up her chin, there was just the hint of a smile on her mouth.

Michael leaned down and pressed his lips to hers, gently at first, exploring the curve of her lips, their petallike softness. But the feel of her was so longed-for that it was not a first kiss, but rather a sort of rejoining, and he pressed more eagerly now, his tongue gaining entrance so he could taste the sweetness of her mouth.

Cathy pulled away first, her hands pressing reluctantly against his chest. "Ummmm, enough," she said softly, her words barely audible over the beating of her heart.

Michael looked down at her, breathing quickly. "I'm afraid I took advantage of the moment. Sorry. I didn't mean to frighten you—"

"No." Cathy tried to control her trembling. "No, frightened is *not* the word I'd use right now. And that's why we'd better stop."

She slid forward and stood up in front of him, then turned and placed one hand on his shoulder to steady herself, feeling giddy. "Well, Michael Winters, this has been . . . unbelievable, but I think I better get back."

"Back?" For a moment Michael did not know what she was talking about, and then the heat of the moment cooled and reality snapped into focus. She meant back to shore.

"In my robe?" he asked quickly. "Your clothes aren't even dry yet."

Cathy looked down at herself and laughed. "You're right, of course. Maybe there are extras on the boat? I'd return them."

Michael did not answer. Instead, he reached for his wineglass, letting his mind leap ahead to the evening's agenda, the gala party in the salon. And small talk. And interviews for the follow-up story. And pictures. They were sure to want more of those, though he had had enough pictures taken to last a lifetime. Damn, just too many hours left to get through. And this woman? She would vanish as quickly as she had appeared.

"Michael?"

He had been gearing up, making plans. "Sorry, you were saying—?"

She gave him a quizzical look. "I was saying I'm going to take a look at my clothes and then I'll have to decide—"

"Right. About leaving." He nodded. That was what was supposed to happen next.

But when she closed the door behind her, he picked up the phone, gave a terse message to the captain, and hung up.

Cathy came out carrying her thin sundress. "Well,

it's not so bad, Michael. I mean, it's still a little wet, but who's going to see me?"

"Cathy—"

"I think if I shake it a little," she said, loosening the dress in her hands, "it'll be okay."

"Cathy, I want to talk about this—"

"Do you hear that?" she interrupted, her head tipping toward the outside door.

"Yes, that's what—"

"We must be heading into shore! I'd better hurry!" Throwing open the door, she stepped out and rushed to the railing.

Michael hurried after her. "Cathy, let me explain!"

But it was too late. She was leaning against the railing, her hands gripping the cold metal rung. Even in the shadowed lights of the deck he could see her face grow pale.

Cathy stared in shock. The tiny pinpoints of light that indicated land were fading fast behind them. Ahead, behind, all around as far as she could see, there was nothing but the churning black waters of the Atlantic Ocean.

Three

"Michael," Cathy shouted, "we're going the wrong way. Stop the boat!"

Michael looked calmly at her. The wind was whipping her brown curls around her cheeks and her pretty face was flushed with anger. And the fact that she had called this million-dollar oceangoing yacht a boat seemed the only point worth commenting on. "She's called a ship, Cathy."

"Unbelievable!" Cathy groaned. Her fingers clung to the railing and she yelled at him above the roar of the engines. "I don't care if you call it a duck, Michael, do something!"

"I did." He leaned down and try to direct his words into her ear. "I told them to get this thing moving or I'd never make my meeting in the Abacos tomorrow."

"What?" Cathy yelled. Her hands flew to her head now as she tried unsuccessfully to press the flying curls back against her scalp. The robe flapped wildly against her body.

Michael took her by the elbow and steered her back into the stateroom, closing the door behind them. "I said," he repeated slowly, "that we're going to the Abaco Islands. I have a meeting there tomorrow morning."

Cathy's eyes widened even more. "The Albatross Islands—" Her voice began to rise. "I never heard of them. And *I* don't have a meeting there, wherever there is!"

"Abacos," Michael said in the same quiet, controlled voice. It was the same voice that won him million-dollar deals, surely it would calm Cathy Stephenson. "It's an interesting place, Cathy. You'll like it."

Cathy stared at him as if he had two heads. The man was incredible. He was the most conceited, arrogant . . . the most handsome, kind . . .

She squeezed her eyes closed for a minute and wished for an ounce of Gap's wonderful patience. Then she opened them narrowly. "Listen, Michael Bradford Winters, I don't care if you're meeting the President or the Pope or Bonnie Prince Charlie there—"

"Actually, he's a sheikh," Michael interrupted.

"I want to go home!" Cathy's voice bounced around the stateroom. Her eyes blazed furiously. "You have no right to do this. It's kidnapping, it's abduction, it's—"

"Expedient." He shrugged. "You'll be able to get a flight home from the Abacos more easily than finding a rental car in the middle of the night. And it fits my plans."

"Oh, good." Cathy snapped. She folded her arms

across her chest and made herself count to ten. Think it through. Be rational. Here she was on a yacht. On her way to goodness knows where. With strangers.

Well, not *complete* strangers, not considering the last few hours. The man *had* saved her life—and done several interesting things since then.

"Michael," she said softly, "I appreciate what you've done for me, I really do. I'm sorry I lost my temper. I'm sure from your vantage point, my troubles must seem insignificant. Easily solved. You rescued me. And I do owe you my life, truly. But right now I've got to get back to Orlando and decide what to do and find a different job and try to patch everything back together. Can't you understand?"

Her eyes were huge again, dark as sweet chocolate, asking nothing but a way back home.

Michael looked away. "Listen, Cathy, why not think of this as just a little detour? A one-day excursion? I promise, on my honor—" He placed his palm flat against his broad chest and Cathy followed the movement with her eyes, remembering the feel of that chest when he had held her.

"Honor?" She echoed weakly.

He misunderstood. "Hell yes. In spite of what you might think, Cathy, I *am* an honorable man. And I *will* get you back to Orlando." He glanced at his watch. "But right now I have to go. There's a party that got under way a while ago, and since I am the guest of honor, I'd better change these clothes and make an appearance."

"Yes, you'd better," Cathy acquiesced, her thoughts already unraveling like so many loose threads. Maybe if he left she'd be able to clear her head, figure all this out.

Michael had his hand on the door. "Listen, why don't you rest for a while and then come on up to the main salon? You'll enjoy yourself."

Before she could respond, he was gone. His faint musky smell remained, mingled with oiled teak and the tang of the sea. Cathy shivered. Then she flopped down on the couch and pulled the terry robe tightly around her. "Tired as I am, I can't be dreaming," she said softly. "You don't smell things in dreams, do you?" She rested her head against the back of the leather sofa, sighed, and closed her eyes. "Oh, Gap, if you could see me now."

A crisp knock on the inside door of the cabin startled her awake. "Yes?" she said.

"Mr. Winters sent me, ma'am," a man's voice said. "He sent down some clothes."

Cathy made sure her robe was fastened tightly before she hurried to the door. Clothes, great. Now she could get out of this robe and into something else, a nice warm pair of sweats, maybe. She pulled open the door and smiled brightly at the uniformed young man who stood straight and tall in front of her. He held a hanger wrapped in blue plastic.

"Thanks a lot. I appreciate it." She stepped aside and he walked in and laid the bag flat across the couch.

"Anything else, ma'am?" he asked. "I'm Bradley, and Mr. Winters said I should watch out for you and bring you anything you want."

"Do you have a taxi?" Seeing the confused expression on his face, she laughed and patted him on his sleeve. "Just a joke. Nope, I think I'm fine."

"Good night, then, ma'am." Bradley tipped his head politely and Cathy fought the impulse to salute back. The second the door closed behind her, she began to tear the plastic covering off the clothes.

"Good grief!"

Gingerly she lifted the silky garment from the wraps and stared at it. It slipped across her fingers like tinsel from a Christmas tree.

This definitely was not for sleeping in, nor would it pass for exercise clothes—at least not for the kind of exercise she'd had in mind! Cathy moaned. The man was outrageous!

But it *was* gorgeous, the most elegant dress, in fact, that Cathy had ever seen. She imagined an actress wearing it to an opening night, or maybe a movie star to the Oscars, where everyone would point and screech and the next day there'd be a million replicas flooding the market. This one was surely an original, that much was apparent even to Cathy's untrained eye. She held it up and glanced at an oval mirror next to the door. The dress was midnight-blue silk. When light fell onto the fabric, the color changed in places, deepening or lightening into streaks of shimmering midnight sky.

Cathy swayed slightly, and the dress slid luxuriously against her body. Who would wear a gown like this? Someone glamorous, exciting, interesting. But not an assistant editor—*ex–assistant editor,* to be more precise—from Bloomington, Indiana.

Cathy put the dress back on the hanger and hung

it on a brass hook behind the door. So much for elegance. She sank back down into the cushions. Why was she so surprised, she wondered. He *was* Michael Bradford Winters, multimillionaire, jet-setter, real-estate tycoon, *and* the Great American Bachelor. The tabloids did not call him that for nothing. What did you expect him to send you, Stephenson? A pair of jeans and a pizza? Ha!

At the thought of food, her stomach made a long, indelicate sound that Cathy thought might be misjudged as a foghorn if anyone had been walking past her door. She pushed both hands over it. "Silence," she scolded.

Food! Cathy looked around. There was a cabinet full of brandies and a can of peanuts. She opened the small refrigerator. Olives, soda, anchovies. She scowled and let it fall shut. Here they were in Florida and there was no fruit! No, scratch that, she thought. Here they were *leaving* Florida, crossing the ocean, going to someplace she could not pronounce. It all made her head ache.

She padded over to the door and opened it a crack. The hallway was dimly lit, thickly carpeted, and empty. Cathy took a few steps out and looked around. It was as elegant as a fine hotel. Beautiful paintings hung on the walls and low brass lights illuminated the paisley pattern in the carpet. At one end of the hallway were wide steps, and Cathy could hear faint music, laughter, the clinking of glasses. But mostly she could smell food. Maybe if she could make her stomach happy, she'd be able to think more clearly and come up with a way out of this mess.

She slipped back into her stateroom and closed

the door. "You do what you have to do," she murmured to herself. How many times had Gap preached that to her as a child? Well, maybe there was some truth to it.

Cathy untied the thick robe and let it fall to the carpet. She stared at the blue gown hanging from the back of the door. Finally, her fingers shaking, she slipped it from the hanger and over her head.

"Oh, my goodness." Her hands shot up to her breasts. They were very much there, and a goodly portion was exposed for the world to pass judgment on. Cathy was no prude, and certainly wasn't naive, but there weren't a lot of women running around in clothes like this in Indiana.

She turned and looked at herself in the mirror. The dress *was* beautiful. It fit perfectly, flowing over her curves like dark blue honey. The thought made her laugh, and she felt the strain across her breasts. Another slice of skin slipped out.

"That settles it!" she announced to the room in general. "Nice try, Michael Winters, but there is no way on earth I'd be able to eat with this thing on. And that, after all, is the sole reason for my leaving this nice, safe room."

Slipping out of the dress, she tossed it on the couch and began a more careful search, checking drawers and doors she had not opened before.

Finally, inside a mirrored closet in the bathroom, Cathy found an assortment of garments hanging neatly from the rack. Quickly she fingered through them. There were beach robes, slinky nightgowns, bathing suits, and bathrobes. Just when Cathy was about to despair and settle for olives and peanuts, her fingers touched on a silky red shirt. She pulled it out. Attached to the back of the hanger was a pair of loose, flowing pants. "Yes!"

She took one last glance at the elegant dress lying on the couch. These lounging pajamas were not even in the same league, and certainly not appropriate for the kind of party that "the Dress" would attend. But just then her stomach interrupted again, giving a long, forlorn growl of starvation, and her mind was made up.

In minutes Cathy stood in the hallway in the red silk pajamas and a pair of borrowed sandals. She had run a comb through her tangle of curls, pinched her cheeks, wet her lips, and was ready. She looked up the wide carpeted steps. From the delicious odors wafting down the staircase, food was but a few steps away. A tingle of excitement raced through her. An Adventure, she thought, and with a capital A! She might as well follow Gap's advice and make the most of it.

She crept up the steps and rounded a corner. Ahead of her, through a wide doorway, was the grand salon. It filled one end of the yacht and was framed by panel after panel of curved windows that looked out onto the mystery of the sea. Inside all was elegance.

Her eyes widened. It was lovely. Amazing. A room like this floating right in the middle of the ocean. Over two dozen elegantly dressed people milled around holding drinks that were constantly being refilled by the stewards. Cathy scanned the room and then her eyes focused on the far side. There, curving along with the windows, was what she was looking for: a linen-draped table holding silver platters of cheeses and fancy fruits, huge, pink shrimp, and thin slices of rare roast beef. Truffles, small cakes, and enough assorted pastries for a small army decorated the end of the table.

Cathy gave her red pajamas a quick glance. Then, realizing that no one was paying her the slightest bit of attention anyway, she skirted the edges of the room and made her way toward the table.

Fortified with a plate filled with food, Cathy found her way to a small couch in a corner. Not far to her left a young man was playing slow, romantic dance music on a baby grand piano. Cathy settled back. Nice. Comfortable. And the food was almost as good as the Nashville House back in Brown County, Indiana.

"People-watching?" the piano player asked during a break.

Cathy nodded and smiled.

"There's plenty to watch," he remarked.

Cathy followed his glance to a woman near the salon doors whose slinky dress was similar to "the Dress," except the dip in front extended all the way to her waist. Each time she laughed at her companion's remarks, the split widened until nearly every inch of her perfect, evenly tanned breasts was exposed.

Cathy blinked, then began a long, curious investigation of the rest of the occupants of the salon, with their easy, elegant gestures, the practiced hugs, and the smiles that seemed to fuse together into one long, upturned line. Beautifully gowned women and handsome men in crisp white shirts and tuxedos flirted and chatted and then collected in small clumps, where their faces took on the serious looks of real estate moguls buying Staten Island.

"Is this your first time on *La Cygne*?" the musician asked.

Cathy grinned at him. "Yes, it is. And my last. I was pulled out of the sea—"

"So *you're* the one," the young man said. "Well, hi. It's a pleasure to meet you. I'm Danny, and *you* were the main topic of conversation at dinner tonight."

"You mean a roomful of sophisticated people like this found nothing better to talk about than me?" Cathy laughed.

"Probably the fact that the man of the hour was your hero helped a little."

"You mean Michael," Cathy said softly.

The piano player nodded toward the far side of the room. "The one and only—"

Again Cathy followed his glance. And then her heart made a funny little jump. Michael had just come in from the promenade deck surrounding the salon. There was a glamorous blonde draped around him like ivy, but Cathy paid her little attention. It was Michael, Michael in his black tuxedo and bow tie, who captured her attention. He looked every inch the magazine's cover story. Michael, with his thick dark hair wind-ruffled and his sea-blue eyes flashing, who stopped her heart.

"Oh, he's handsome," she murmured.

Danny laughed and then shifted on the polished bench and began to play again. Strains of "Stardust" filtered across the room and mixed with the clink of glasses and the party chatter.

Michael's gaze met Cathy's. He stared at her for a long moment, and then smoothly disentangled himself from the woman next to him. With a grace Cathy found mesmerizing, he wound his way through the people to her side.

"I'm glad you came," he said.

"I was hungry." Cathy smiled up at him and lifted her empty plate for him to inspect.

"I see. Would you care for more?" He signaled a steward without waiting for an answer.

"I guess I do," Cathy said with a slight laugh.

"By the way, you look terrific."

Michael had spotted her immediately when he came into the room. She stood out, set apart by her fresh, natural beauty and those brilliant red pajamas. Obviously she'd vetoed the dress he'd sent! The thought had amused him, and then right on top of it he had felt a stirring of desire so strong it propelled him across the room to her side.

"Thanks for sending that dress," Cathy was blushing and explaining, "but I just couldn't do it. It was beautiful, I'll grant you that, but I'm afraid I would have wobbled in here so self-consciously that my shaking would have caused it to fall right off."

"I like your choice," he answered softly.

She had been talking too fast and now she had to draw a quick little breath. It was because he was so close. If he gave her a little breathing room, she would feel much better.

She slid over on the bench toward the piano and put her plate down next to her. "Would you like to sit down?" she asked, pointing to the other side of her plate.

"For a minute." He settled down and stretched his long legs out in front of him. "Then I should take you around and introduce you to people."

"Why?"

Michael shrugged. Why indeed? What he'd *like* to do right then was carry her off to his stateroom and keep her all to himself. That would give all those reporters something to write about. But it would also scare the hell out of Cathy Stephenson, and he had no intention of doing that—yet. Instead, he thought back to her question. "Because I'm sure they'd like to meet you."

"Oh, I *don't* think so," Cathy quipped without the slightest hesitation. "Do you know what I have in common with these people, Michael? The shrimp, that's what. We all nibbled on the same batch of shrimp. That's about it."

"Is that fair? You might have thought that of me, but we've found a lot to talk about."

Cathy looked at him candidly. "Unusual circumstances, Mr. Winters. If our paths had crossed in any other way, on the streets of any city or even at adjacent tables in some restaurant, we would never have spoken two words to each other."

"Lucky for me things worked out as they did."

She smiled, dazzled by his compliment, then had another thought. "You know, I don't think luck can really be given any of the credit. From what I've seen of you, and the little I've read, you *make* things happen." Her smile slid into a wry grin. "My being here right this moment certainly proves that."

"You're not angry anymore?"

She laughed. "Not at this instant."

Around them the party ebbed and swirled. The gaiety, the noise, the cocktail talk, were just a faint annoyance on the periphery of Michael's vision. He was watching her.

And Cathy was watching him. "Why don't you like parties?" she asked him. "Especially when you're the guest of honor?"

"Who says I don't?" he asked, one dark brow dipping low in consternation.

She laughed softly, dropping her hands on his shoulders. "Your whole body says it wants to be somewhere else, out of that tux. And the way your brow swoops—"

"Swoops?"

"Swoops," she repeated firmly. "And the way you glare when the noise gets too loud. I hope you have more of a poker face when you're negotiating a business deal."

That comment made him laugh out loud. "I seem to do all right."

"Glad to hear it." She grinned at him. She accepted the plate the waiter brought and looked delightedly at the assortment of tiny sandwiches. "You know, swimming in the ocean really makes you hungry. Want some?"

"No thanks."

"Good!"

He laughed again, then cut it short. One of the things reporters liked to dwell on was his "brooding look," as they called it. Enigmatic. Inscrutable. "The Unknowable Michael Bradford Winters," they had dubbed him. If they saw him with Miss Indiana laughing like a college freshman they would be crushed. And *that* thought made him laugh again. He shook his head. "Cathy, you're wonderful."

Cathy stopped eating long enough to frown at him. "What a strange thing to say. Interesting, I'd buy. Or charming," she teased. "But wonderful? Compared to all this, my life is very ordinary. *I'm* a very ordinary person. That's how they grow 'em in Indiana."

"Believe me, what you've done to a weekend I was beginning to find suffocating is definitely extraordinary. And that makes you quite wonderful."

"Which reminds me of something not so wonderful." Cathy put down her plate. "And that's this predicament. Now that I've eaten, I want to figure this out."

"It's no problem and it's all figured out. We get to the Abacos tomorrow morning. I have some business to attend to and you can be off to Orlando on a plane if that's what you want. You'll be home by bedtime."

"Just like that?" Cathy fell quiet.

A whole carload of emotions barreled around inside her, but that sharp stab of disappointment threw her for a loop. Blame it on him! Michael Winters's world was too fast for her. The easy commands, the snapping of fingers and having things appear and disappear, the total disregard of things like the cost of her plane ticket and the fact that she had probably lost her job, her instantly replaceable wardrobe—all that shadowed her heart-stopping excitement with confusion.

She shook her head.

But before she could speak, he rose. "Excuse me a moment, will you?"

"Certainly."

Now she was free to catch her breath. She sat and watched him as he stood talking nearby with a group of men. It was fascinating. They all wore ad-perfect tans and seemed to be forceful and confident, with deep, commanding voices and sure gestures. Yet, Cathy decided, each paled a little next to Michael. He had presence. And the women . . . *they* all seemed determined to seduce the Great American Bachelor. Oh, well, Cathy thought, that was probably to be expected. After all, his title wasn't the *celibate* bachelor! Certainly a man like Michael Winters had been around the block a time or two.

But still, with the tiniest flicker of jealousy, she was happy to see how cool his response was. He treated each one exactly the same: with polite, gracious indifference. Maybe he was just tired tonight. She grinned to herself. After all, saving someone's life was bound to take something out of a person!

"Any requests?" the piano player asked.

She had forgotten about Danny, but now he was leaning toward her, smiling.

"How about 'Good Night, Ladies'?" Cathy said.

"I don't think the fine folks would appreciate that; the party is still young."

"But not for me." Cathy stood, smiled at him, and stifled a yawn. "I'm beat. It's been a busy day."

"That's the understatement of the decade," the young man said. "Unless you drive cars into oceans frequently."

Cathy shook her head. "I try to keep it down to two or three a year." She yawned again, and they both laughed.

"G'night, Danny." She waved at the young man and wandered across the room.

She decided to take the outside route back to the stateroom and let the ocean lull her on the way. Slipping through the open door, she saw that the wide wedge of deck outside the salon was softly lit with lanterns and scattered couples were standing or sitting in shadows, enjoying the evening air. The wavering lights lit her way as she walked over to the railing and looked out across the water.

It was incredible. There was nothing but the dark, rolling ocean for as far as she could see. The world she lived in had disappeared completely. Above her a few stars distinguished the sky from the water, but except for that, it was a continuous blanket of deep, thick, impenetrable blackness.

Cathy wrapped her arms around herself and smiled out at the majesty of such vastness. She felt small, insignificant, and strangely at peace.

"You're not thinking of jumping, are you?"

Cathy jumped.

"Sorry." Michael wrapped his arm around her. "Didn't mean to scare you. I saw you head for the door and wanted to make sure you were all right. I didn't mean to leave you earlier, but someone wanted to see me."

"Understandable, since you're the man of the hour." She laughed lightly. But the peace she'd felt a minute before was shattered. Here he was, one arm tossed lightly over her shoulders, and she was undone. The ocean had vanished. The ship had vanished. There was only him, standing so close, his breath on her face. She felt her heart leap and hammer at her throat. Her skin went hot and cold and hot again. She had never felt anything like this fierce desire. It was crazy. Crazy! She was going to have to stop this!

"Are you having a good time?"

"Lovely. The food was delicious, the company charming. And now I'm on my way to bed." She tried to walk away, but his arm stayed firmly around her shoulder. "Michael—"

A flashbulb lit the darkness. "Hey, Michael, there you are!"

Cathy and Michael turned together, and it was a face she recognized from earlier, though she had not noticed the camera then.

"Cathy, this is Nick Mendello with *Time*. He's doing the follow-up story."

Cathy nodded and smiled while Nick pumped her hand, continuing to talk to Michael as he did so. "Michael, I need a couple more shots before I close up shop here. You with a guest would be great. Female, of course."

Michael nodded but Cathy saw the lines of tension tighten around his blue eyes. No poker face now; his annoyance was obvious.

But, holding his temper, he slipped his arm back around Cathy's shoulder and moved so they both faced the camera. "Okay, how's this?"

"Michael, I—"

He overruled her objection. "This'll just take a second."

Nick Mendello shifted his camera, adjusted his lens and looked up again. With a professional glance around, he waved to a woman standing near the doorway.

Cathy recognized her as the woman whose dress had astonished her earlier.

"Michael, why don't you put your arm around the countess there?"

Cathy could feel Michael's anger ignite. "Mendello, don't bother Fran. I said to take *this* shot—" He pulled her closer.

"I just thought . . ." Mendello began. "I mean no offense, ma'am," he said, bobbing his head toward Cathy, "but this shot'll go with the party spread. I thought they might want someone more—"

Sophisticated? Cathy finished in her head. Beautiful? She could feel the flush of her own anger rising in her throat.

". . . recognizable," the photographer finished lamely, but Michael cut him off.

"I want her."

Cathy had had just about enough of the two of them! Dying of embarrassment, she tugged free of Michael's encircling arm. "Did either of you think of asking whether I want my picture taken?"

"Cathy, I just—" He touched her arm.

"The answer is no, I don't want my picture taken!" Her piercing gaze flicked between Michael and the photographer, and then settled for another brief moment on Michael. "And furthermore"—she poked one finger into his starched tuxedo shirt—"I don't know how you usually operate, but I am not about to take orders from you. Good night!"

Before Michael or Nick could speak, she was gone, a red streak through the black night.

Four

At dawn the next morning, a candy-striped light-house was shining out over a turquoise sea.

The sight made Cathy gasp in delight. This was not Indiana. Not anything she had ever seen before, or even imagined. This was a fairy tale.

As the yacht cut a wide, curling wake through the Atlantic, dolphins lured from the deep jumped and leapt in pairs like ballet dancers on tailfins instead of toe shoes. A flash of silver and a wide, dark eye, and they disappeared behind the ship. Cathy leaned over the rail for one more look, just a glimpse to freeze in memory. "Hello!" she called. "Hello, you beautiful things. Hello—"

Her waving arm drew the gulls, hungry for a hand-out, to whom any lifted arm meant a fish head or a piece of bread. They soared and swooped and soared again, and Cathy covered her head and laughed aloud at their bullying. "Go away, you bandits. Shoo!" she shouted.

No one heard. The captain and crew were at their posts, guiding the ship toward its early morning rendezvous. The guests were all predictably asleep, recovering no doubt from the previous night's party. And Michael was nowhere to be seen.

Which was fine with Cathy.

A lovely night's sleep, accompanied by the comforting lullaby of the engines and the gentle rocking of the ship, had chased away all her annoyance. How could anyone be angry at anything on a morning like this, she mused happily. And when would she ever get another chance to step inside a fairy tale like this? But she was not quite ready to let Michael Winters off the hook. Let him think she was still furious. Let him think she disapproved. Let him think . . .

She laughed aloud, a soft, musical sound of rippling notes that winged across the water. If he thought of her at all, it would be a miracle! More likely he was sound asleep in a not-so-empty bed, or getting ready for his big business deal. She shrugged. She was not the kind of girl to get her feelings hurt by fairy-tale princes on yachts *or* shining white horses. She was a practical Indiana farm girl who knew the salt wind in her face was a gift she should enjoy while it lasted. So she did.

She wandered from bow to stern, from leeward to starboard, not knowing a single nautical term but enjoying every step. A steward scared the life out of her by materializing without a sound at her elbow with a steaming cup of coffee, but the coffee was wonderful, freshly brewed and flavored with cinnamon, and she thanked him profusely. From then on she kept a semi-watchful eye on the portholes and hatches, but no one else was stirring.

Shading her eyes with the flat of one hand, she checked the sun. "Cock crow or earlier," she decided. Six-thirty, maybe seven. Early. A lovely, early, have-the-world-all-to-yourself time.

"A penny for your thoughts?"

The husky, not yet familiar sound of Michael's voice caused her to spin her around. A grin tugged at one corner of his mouth. "A dollar, then. Deal?"

"My thoughts are my own, to keep or give away." She tipped her head, wide eyes shining. "But you're welcome to my observations."

"If they have to do with last night, I think I'd rather pass."

Cathy blinked. Did he really care what she thought, this man of contradictions, this gorgeous playboy, this confirmed bachelor? Or was this just a move in a game she had never played? Hiding her thoughts behind a smile sweet as a Hershey kiss, she answered, "These are strictly early morning observations. Minted fresh with the sunrise."

"Okay. Then I'm ready. What does an Indiana girl see here?" He swept an arm out to the horizon.

Cathy leaned both arms on the rail and rested her chin in her hands. "I see dolphins dancing on the waves, and waves tossed by the wind, each wearing little white bonnets with their strings flying loose behind, and more colors of blue and green than I ever thought existed. What *makes* all those blues?"

she mused, pointing a slim hand down toward the water.

"Water currents. Rivers that flow through the ocean just as rivers do on land. And changes in depth. There are mountains down there, and valleys. Plains. Outcroppings of coral and huge reefs made from the minuscule bodies of millions of tiny creatures." His voice was soft yet powerful, and so utterly serious that Cathy turned to look at him.

He loved this, she realized with a start. Something here was special to him. Cherished. Whether he admitted it or not.

Feeling her gaze on his face, Michael turned. His grin was sudden, boyish, and unexpected. "Hey, you're supposed to be looking *out there*. And *you're* supposed to be doing the talking. That was the deal."

"And I'd never welsh on a bargain." She grinned back. "Observation number two: We are definitely heading for that island, the one with the candy-cane lighthouse, which suits me just fine, since I've never seen anything so pretty. Oh—" She squinted into the distance. "It's not just one island, is it? More like a string of beads on a necklace, pearls in a turquoise sea . . ."

"Cays," he said, pronouncing it "keys."

"Ah. Cays. And do they have names?"

"Together they're called the Abacos. It's a chain of islands curving about one hundred thirty miles north to south, from Walker's Cay to Hole-in-the-Wall."

"Great name!"

"There's more: Strangers Cay, Green Turtle Cay and Whale Cay, Treasure Cay, and that, right ahead of us, is Hope Town."

"That's a nice destination." She nodded, smiling at the rightness of it.

"Optimist!"

"Maybe." She laughed. "But if you think I'm going to start singing 'I'm as corny as Kansas in August . . .' you're mistaken."

"Wrong ocean," he teased.

"Wrong girl." She tossed him a wink.

"Okay, so at least I know they have theater in Indiana."

"They have everything in Indiana."

"Not islands."

"No," she conceded, "not islands. And certainly not tropical islands with palm trees and white sandy beaches. Which makes it a perfect ending for my adventure."

"I'm glad you're satisfied."

"Oh, I am!"

"Good. And you'll be glad to be heading home?"

"Of course."

"Good."

He stuffed his hands in the pockets of his trousers and stared out at the ocean, frowning. "So . . ."

"Sew a stitch," she quipped, and a grin stole up to her sparkling eyes. "That was one of Gap's favorite sayings whenever *I* stood around and sulked."

His jaw dropped. "I am not sulking."

"Oh. Pardon me. It must be one of those high-powered stress-induced mood swings I've read so much about in *Psychology Today*." Her chin trembled with laughter. "Of course," she added as though to the gulls, "back home in Indiana we call it sulking."

"I—am—not—sulking."

"No. Now you're yelling."

"I am not yelling," he insisted, and though his eyes were fierce, the corner of his mouth had twitched up in a grin. He stared at her, eyes narrowed, his gaze jumping across her eyes, mouth, cheeks, chin, forehead. As if his eyes were steel and her face a magnet.

Cathy let him look, refusing to acknowledge the heat that rushed to her cheeks. Why, if she were granted a wish, she would find out what it was like to fall in love with a man like this. She would let her heart pound like a drum, and feel her blood surge like the tide. She would step inside the fairy tale, all right. After all, Cinderella *did* marry the prince. . . .

"What are you thinking?" he demanded, his gaze locked on hers now.

"None of your business," she answered, spinning around and laughing up at the gulls.

Michael stepped up behind her and wrapped his arms around her waist. "Tell me," he whispered in her hair. "Tell me."

The heat of his breath sent shivers racing down her spine. Her nipples tingled and her knees went weak. Crazy! She thought. This is crazy, some game he plays.

"Tell me."

Crazy. Crazy. She turned in his arms and looked up into his face. There was something, something in his eyes, some feeling, some need glimpsed like a fish in deep blue seas . . . something reaching for her. . . .

Before she knew she would, she rose on tiptoe and

kissed him, fitting her mouth to his, tasting his lips, his breath, his sweetness.

Michael was too surprised to kiss her back. In a second she had pulled away and the salt breeze was on his lips where her kiss had been, and his throat was dry. He stared at her. It was as if the sun had risen at night, or the ship leapt up and sailed through the sky. The world had gone mad.

"Sorry," she said, eyes round as marbles. "Sorry!" She started to laugh with embarrassment, her shoulders shaking. "I am so sorry. I don't know what made me do that."

"Don't be sorry." His voice was rough and low.

"But I am! I'm not that forward. Honest I'm not."

"That's not what I think—"

"Then you must think I'm crazy."

Laughing at her echo of his own thoughts, he answered, "Crazy, yes. Crazy and wonderful. Cathy—" He caught her in his arms and pulled her tight against him, the narrowness of her trapped within the circle of his arms. "Cathy—"

"Michael." She struggled, flattening her palms against his chest. "Forget it ever happened! Let me go."

"No. I don't want to."

"Michael." She gasped, half laughing, half frowning, "This doesn't make any sense."

"For once I don't care. For once I don't want to make sense. I don't want to be logical and calculating, weighing all the possible gains and losses. Not this time. For once maybe it doesn't have to make sense to be right."

"That doesn't sound like the Michael Winters I

saw last night," she teased, tipping her head back to watch the play of light on his face.

He tightened his hold. "Good! Then maybe—"

A door clicked shut behind them. "Mr. Winters? Excuse me."

Michael spun away, his body tense, his face wiped blank.

It was the first mate, eyes dropped politely to the deck.

"Yes? What is it?" Michael demanded.

"Fax for you, sir." He held it out in a sealed envelope.

"Thank you. Excuse me one minute, Cathy." He ripped open the envelope and scanned the message. His dark brows furrowed in concentration.

"Bad news?" Cathy asked.

"What?" His eyes flicked to her face. "No. Just a confirmation of a meeting. No problem. And there will be no reply," he added to the mate. "Thank you."

He folded the fax and slipped it into his pocket. "So . . . where were we?"

"Heading into Hope Town," she answered, her eyes lit with amusement.

"That's not what I meant, and you know it." He had moved nearer, near enough for his breath to stir the hair at her temples as he leaned down, near enough for her to feel his heat through his shirt. "Let's try that again, Cathy. This time I'll lead—"

"And we should get in about half a waltz before they throw the anchor. No, Michael." She slipped out from under his arm and leaned back against the rail. "I'm not a half-a-waltz kind of person."

He studied her like a contract, top to bottom, reading every detail, eyes cool and evaluating. Then he shoved his hands deep into his pockets, drew a breath, and smiled. "Take a later plane, Cathy. Meet me for lunch when I'm done with my meeting. Will you?"

The first mate stepped back into sight. " 'Scuse me, sir. Captain asked me to tell you—"

"Just a minute." Michael waved him to silence. "Will you, Cathy? Please?"

She wanted to argue, or at least explain why it was silly. The earliest plane out was the one to catch. Get home. Find a job. Leave this dream behind her. But he had a presence, a power that flowed like an invisible electric current from him, through the salt air and up through her fingertips and from the soles of her feet straight to the back of her skull. Zap! She could not think. Could not argue in front of this wide-eyed first mate even if she got her thoughts together. She opened her mouth to say no. "All right," she said softly.

"Good," he said, and then turned around. "Yes? The message?"

"We'll be docking in ten minutes, sir. Less now."

"Thank you. I'm ready." When the mate left, he swung his electric-blue gaze back to her face. "And thank *you*, Cathy. I'll meet you at noon over at Marsh Harbor. I already had the captain wire ahead for some clothes for you, so you can take your time here on board, or look around Hope Town, and then someone will bring you over to the restaurant in one of the small boats."

"But what if your meeting runs late—"

"It won't."

"What if you get tied up?" she insisted, picturing herself marooned on this tropical island with a yachtful of the rich and famous.

"I'll untie myself." He laughed. "Don't worry, I'll be there."

"I'm not worried."

"Good." His teeth flashed in a reckless grin. "And you won't be sorry."

Did that come with a guarantee, Cathy wondered as the ship swung sharply to port on its final approach to the harbor. The captain sounded the ship's horn, and the cabin doors slid open to a sudden flurry of reporters and photographers. Cathy was swept aside by the rush and babble.

"Mr. Winters, can we come along for a quick interview with the sheikh?"

"No."

"How about just a few pictures?"

"No."

"We won't—"

"I said no. *This is business.*"

Without another word Michael spun on his heel and stalked inside. The crowd followed.

Cathy was suddenly left alone . . . just her and the candy-striped lighthouse guarding the entrance to Hope Town. The engine quieted to a purr. The yacht nudged gently into its slip. Everything else could have been a dream, some waking fantasy of Michael and the kiss and the promise. Was it a dream? Had any of it happened?

Moments later his dark head appeared below as,

with long, smooth strides, he stepped off the yacht and across the wooden pier to a waiting car.

Cathy leaned out and waved, already smiling, certain he would turn and look for her up on deck. He never turned. He vanished into the car and was gone.

"Oh, my," she whispered to the gulls, feeling foolish and transparent. "Caught with my hand in the cookie jar!" Heart thumping, she hurried back to her cabin.

She would call her credit card company, call the airport, arrange a flight. She would leave a note, go back to Orlando, where she belonged. *And never see him again?* The thought sent her heart tumbling to her feet. That would happen soon enough. Why hurry it along?

Instead, she lingered in the bath, dawdled over breakfast. Then there was a steward at the door with an array of boxes, and she spent the next half hour trying on clothes. She settled on a sundress in hand-painted cotton, a pair of sandals to replace those the sea had stolen, and a wide straw hat. Standing in front of the mirror, she looked very islandish, not at all like herself. Feeling carefree, she went up on deck.

The first mate materialized at once. " 'Morning, ma'am. Mr. Winters asked me to take you over to Marsh Harbor in the Whaler before noon."

"He did?"

"Yes, ma'am. Those are my orders."

He was so formal, he made her nervous.

"Well, I—I was just going to wander around for a

while. Take a look at the lighthouse, maybe walk down on the beach."

All of a sudden *he* was looking nervous.

"Don't worry," she assured him, "I'll be back on time. We wouldn't want to keep Mr. Winters waiting."

"No, ma'am, we wouldn't. I'll have the boat ready at eleven forty-five."

"That's fine. Thanks." And then she made a quick escape.

She spent the next hour strolling around the light-house. She shaded her eyes against the bright tropical sun, read the historical markers, marveled at the vivid profusion of flowers. The sun was warm on her head and shoulders, and her skin prickled with anticipation.

"Ms. Stephenson?"

It was the first mate, polite but determined.

"Oh, hi! How are you?"

"Fine, ma'am," he said, touching his cap. "We're running a few minutes late."

"Are we? Sorry. The time just flew. I've never seen any place so pretty."

"The Whaler is tied up back at the pier, ma'am."

"Okay. I'm ready. Let's go." Holding on to her hat, she hurried to keep up with his quick pace.

The poor young man did not say another word, he was so unglued. He helped her into the little out-board, started the engine, and raced them across the crystal-clear waters of Great Abaco Sound. They pulled up to the bustling Boat Harbor Marina and he helped her out and then, holding tight to her elbow as if afraid she'd get away and he'd have to face Michael Winters empty-handed, he hurried her toward the Great Abaco Beach Hotel.

Michael was not there yet, and a little color crept back into the young mate's cheeks. "Here you are, Ms. Stephenson. Have a nice lunch."

He was gone before she could thank him, or ask him to wait in case Michael never showed.

"Oh, well," she said to herself, and followed the hostess to a table near the window. Outside, the sunlight was pouring down upon the street, the marina, and the sound beyond. Incredible! Here she was island-hopping like a pro. Now, where was she? Oh, yes, Marsh Harbor. Was that the name of the town? The cay?

"Excuse me," she ventured as the hostess reappeared with someone's cocktail. "But what is the name of this cay?"

The hostess smiled and placed the drink in front of her. "This is Great Abaco Island," she answered in an English blended of proper British and warm Bahamian. "Think of it as a mother duckling, and the cays are all her little ducks swimming along in a row nearby. And this"—she winked—"is a Bahama Breeze, specialty of the house, and meant to be sipped slowly until Mr. Winters arrives. He regrets his delay."

Cathy chuckled appreciatively. The man did not miss a move. Was someone born knowing exactly the right thing to do at the right time with just the right style? Or did it come during infancy along with milk if one was raised in New York City or Paris or Rio or somewhere equally exotic?

She rested her chin on her palm and looked out the window.

There was Michael Winters, striding down the sidewalk shoulder to shoulder with a sheikh in full flowing robe and head covering, trailed by six narrow-shouldered, slim young men in dark suits and fierce scowls, and they were all turning in at the front.

Cathy caught her breath in amazement.

Before she could let it out again, Michael was there, standing tall beside her chair. "Cathy Stephenson, I'd like to introduce Sheikh Hamoudi. Sheikh, Ms. Cathy Stephenson from Indiana."

"Charmed." The sheikh smiled, kissing her hand.

"The same here." Cathy grinned, wide-eyed and biting back her laughter. "Will you be joining us for lunch?"

Michael's dark brow rose, but the sheikh was already bowing low over her hand. "Thank you, but I must hurry back to the ship. There are arrangements to be made." He turned to Michael. "I will be in touch as soon everything is settled."

"Fine. I enjoyed our meeting."

"As did I. And," he said, his smile reappeared, "Indiana must be lovely place."

He turned and strode out the door, six bodyguards in his wake.

Michael had settled into the seat across from Cathy and was studying her with a mixture of pleasure and amusement. "Sorry about that, but somehow I let slip the fact I was meeting you for lunch, and there was no deterring him."

"Understandable," she teased. "Outside of Indiana, I'm best known here in the Abacos." Her laughter bubbled in her throat like the fizz in fine champagne.

Her eyes sparkled. "Honestly, Michael, why in the world did he drag that whole parade in here?"

"I think it was because I said you were waiting and that I wouldn't be late."

"Ah." She grinned, but her heart was thumping like a big drum. Brass bands marched through her veins. Trumpets sang. "Nice of you, but I wouldn't have minded waiting."

"I was the one who couldn't wait," he said simply.

The silence was lit by the golden sun pouring in the windows, which sat between them, warm and comfortable as a big cat.

"So," he said finally, "how did you like the Bahama Breeze?"

"I didn't taste it," she admitted. "I was waiting for you. For a toast."

"All right." He smiled, signaling the waiter. He looked casually away, around the room, out the window, anywhere but at her face. Until the drink came. Then he looked deep into her eyes, losing himself there.

And suddenly he saw that they weren't just brown but, in this golden light, they were the clear brown of soft earth, of water flowing over dark leaves, of amber shining with inner light. A rich welcoming brown of place, of home.

"Michael!" She blushed. "Are you proposing a toast, or conducting an investigation?"

"A toast!" he assured her, "to"—he thought for a minute—"to tomorrow."

"Tomorrow," she echoed, confused and pleased and wondering.

They tapped glasses and sipped the frothy liquor through their straws.

"Umm-umm!" Cathy nodded, licking her lips. "This is yummy."

"And potent. Have another."

They spent the next hour being silly and happy, ordering too much and tasting each other's food. Michael recommended the locally renowned crawfish salad, and Cathy was in no mood to disagree. Along with homemade sweet potato bread, crunchy fritters, and spicy conch chowder, and a wide, cool slice of key lime pie, she was in heaven. She even tasted Lord knew what from his seafood platter. And it was all the most wonderful food she had ever eaten.

Then he took her sight-seeing.

"Come on," Michael said. He slipped an arm around her waist. "I want to show you everything."

As they walked he told her a little of the history of the islands, how after the American Revolution the Loyalists fled with their slaves to these islands in the Bahamas. How in the mid-1780s a sturdy widow from South Carolina named Malone crossed the ocean with her family, overcame terrible hardships, and founded Hope Town, where they had docked that morning.

"Yes!" Cathy interrupted. "I saw her name on a historical marker there. Now, that's more of an adventure than I could ever handle."

Michael cocked his head. "Don't sell yourself short. I have a feeling you could handle just about anything."

"That's exactly the attitude that got me from Bloomington to Orlando and on into the middle of the ocean, thank you." She shook her head, laughing at herself, making him laugh.

"It's not a bad attitude, despite your recent experiences," he assured her.

"To tell the truth, Michael, my recent experiences haven't all been that bad." Then she pulled her eyes away from his face and looked out over the sound. "So, did Mrs. Malone build the lighthouse?"

"No. The lighthouse wasn't built until almost a hundred years later, and almost caused a riot."

"Why?"

"Because the islanders were making a good living from ships wrecked on the reefs, and they thought a lighthouse would be bad for business."

"How heartless! Can you imagine—" She stopped in mid-sentence and slid him a narrow-eyed, skeptical glance. "Never mind." She sighed heartily. "I *won't* ask what side you would have voted on."

His laughter ruffled the hair at her neck. "Thanks a lot, friend!"

Arm around her waist, he walked her down on the pink sand and up the lovely shaded sidewalks.

"It's a little like New England, where I grew up, but with palm trees," he remarked.

"You like it, don't you?" She smiled, leaning comfortably against the circle of his arm.

"Oh, sure. It's a beautiful spot," he answered lightly.

Surprised, she looked up at him. She had been so entranced by the beauty of the island that she assumed he was as well. And here he was, cool as a cucumber! Oh, well, perhaps if you'd seen all the world . . .

With a shrug she came back to the moment, and to what Michael was saying.

"If you think this is pretty, there's one more place you've got to see."

Without a second's hesitation he took her hand and led her back to the marina.

"We'll be taking the Whaler," he informed the mate. And in moments they were cutting across the turquoise waters of the sound.

The little boat zipped on past large cays and little tiny cays and cays that were just tree-covered bumps breaking the blue surface of the water. Cathy longed to explore, but they did not stop.

Then he slowed the boat and headed for a middle-size island skirted with wide beaches, lush vegetation, and crystal-clear coves. Michael headed into one such cove and pulled up alongside a covered wooden pier. He stepped out and offered her a hand. "Welcome to Yellowtail Cay."

The whole island was just two miles long and a half mile wide, edged with beaches whose sand was soft as baby powder—and *pink*.

"Michael," she cried, kicking off her sandals and burying her feet right up to the ankles. "Pink sand! I've never heard of anything like it."

"It's because of the coral," he explained, walking barefoot beside her. "In Hawaii they have black sand, because of the volcanic origin."

"Must you be so scientific? Tell me it's magic!" She wiggled her toes into the cool sand.

He slipped an arm around her and tugged her close. "Come on, there's more I want you to see." They walked down to the little settlement nestled on the southern end of the cay. The old streets were lined with clapboard houses—pink, yellow, robin's-egg blue, edged with white picket fences and trees bursting with fruit—grapefruit, oranges, limes. There was a narrow restaurant with fans whirling over two tables on the front porch, an equally narrow grocery store that also sold hand-printed cotton shirts and straw bags, and a post office.

A woman sat on the post office step, and she rose to her feet when she saw Michael. "Well, Mr. Winters, I heard you were back in these parts. Come to stay awhile?"

"Hello, Julia." He smiled. "It's good to see you. But no, I'm not staying. Just showing your island off to a friend. This is Cathy Stephenson. Julia Jennings."

"*Your* island, Mr. Winters," the woman corrected him with laughing eyes as she offered Cathy a good, strong handclasp. Cathy liked her immediately, her eyes dark as India ink, her hair braided and beaded in beautiful, intricate patterns. "So, what do you think of our little place?"

"I think it's heavenly!" Cathy's gaze touched on everything in sight. "The trees, the beaches, the houses—I was just picturing my grandmother rocking on a porch like that," she admitted, then the color rose to her cheeks.

"Well, looks like your friend might want a nice long iced tea." Julia smiled. "And I've got to get me back to work. Good seeing you, Mr. Winters." She climbed the steps and turned. "Soon come!" she called out the local, lilting good-bye that encouraged return, then she vanished inside.

"So, you do like it?" Michael asked as they took seats on the restaurant porch.

"Like it? I love it. I meant what I said. I can picture Gap and Aunt Tisha, dressed in wide cotton skirts, looking for shells on those pink beaches, or sitting on the porch of a pink house, in a wooden swing, eating an orange from the tree outside their door. And to think that if I climbed to the post office roof, I could see the Sound so calm on one side and the Atlantic roaring on the other." She lifted both shoulders in amazement. "Why, it's as close to paradise as *I've* ever seen."

"It's that sheltered life you've led." He winked at her. Leaning back, he drummed his fingers on the tabletop.

Cathy tipped her head and gave him another of her long, searching glances. "Michael, what did Julia mean about *your* island? Do you have a home here?"

"No. She meant the island."

"You own it?" Cathy's heart skipped a beat.

"Yes."

"You bought it? How? When?"

"I don't remember the details of the transaction. It was years ago."

"But you own the whole island?"

"It isn't a very big island, as properties go."

"But it's"—she waved her hands around to draw it all close, struggling to find the words she wanted— "it's . . . it's like a whole little world. Complete. Perfect."

Michael looked suddenly uncomfortable. "It's a piece of real estate, Cathy. Just a place."

"Oh, Michael!" She waved a hand at him as if he were crazy, laughing at the absurdity of it. "Every place is just a place, but some are special, they talk to you, they claim you."

He folded his arms across his chest, silent.

Realizing that she may have said too much, Cathy quickly changed the subject, chattering on about the palms and the flowers and the birds. After all, this wasn't her island. This wasn't her man. What did she know about it all? The fact that it touched her in some special way had nothing to do with reality. He had brought her to see the island, which was lovely of him. And when she went back to Indiana for Christmas, she would tell them all about this man she had met and his Yellowtail Cay.

They drank iced teas with slices of lime still warm from the tree. And they walked back along the beach, kicking up the warm sand with their toes, leaving their footprints behind to be washed away by the tide. Holding her shoes in one hand, her hat in the other, she stepped down into the Whaler and sat looking over her shoulder as the boat pulled away and the island slid back to the horizon. *Soon come,* she thought. Good-bye!

Two of the dark-suited, scowling young men were waiting for them back at the marina at Marsh Harbor. On the other side of the street stood a serious older man dressed in a somber suit, carrying a briefcase. "My accountant," Michael explained shortly, throwing the rope to the first mate. He helped Cathy out of the boat and guided her across the street with one cool hand at her elbow. "Yes, Roger?"

"The deal is complete, sir. Everything in order.

Papers ready to be signed. The sheikh is waiting upstairs."

"Cathy"—Michael turned to her—"I'm sorry, but I've got just a few minutes worth of business to tie up. Would you like a drink while you wait?"

Cathy smiled. "Two Bahama Breezes a day is my limit! I'll just stroll on down the pier and look at the boats . . . ooops, ships," she corrected herself. "Take your time; don't worry about me."

And in truth it took very little time. Ten minutes, and he was back, coming up behind her so quietly that she could feel his breath on her neck even as he brushed a light kiss there. "Hi."

"Hi yourself! You scared me."

"Not my intention at all," he assured her, his eyes blazing.

"So you took care of business?"

"Yes."

"What big deal did you tie up?" she asked, smiling up at him in that half-teasing, half-serious way of hers.

He paused for just a second too long. Then, as if it meant nothing, he answered coolly, "I sold the island."

Five

"Sold it?" Cathy echoed.

"Yes. I got a good price."

"But . . ." Cathy struggled for words, too stunned to speak. The words rattled around in her head, accusing, disbelieving, heartbroken, but there was nothing to say. Nothing.

"Oh, my . . ." she whispered. "I guess I just don't know anything about your world. I—I—" Stupid tears jumped to her eyes, and she turned to look out over the water, determined not to let him see.

"Cathy, are you upset?" Michael sounded honestly surprised.

"Of course not." She tossed her head, blinking hard. Striving for composure, she turned to face him. "No, I'm not upset, and it's nothing for you to worry about. In my life things go slower. I mean, a family can save up all their lives just to buy a little *house*, and then they'll probably look around for months, and once they have it it's home and they never give it up. They settle in. They love it. I don't know—" She laughed, at herself really. "The thought of you trading away that island without a blink . . . it leaves me breathless. And frightened somehow."

She shook her head, her mouth crimped with dismay though she fought for composure. "Michael, that was your island, your choice. It has nothing to do with me."

He rocked back on his heels, shoulders set. "Cathy, business is business. That's all. That's what I do for a living: buy real estate, sell real estate, take a piece of land and see an opportunity, see what it could be developed into in the future."

She looked up into his eyes. "But it was perfect now, Michael," she answered simply.

He did not answer. A muscle jumped along his jaw, and his eyes were dark and unreadable. She had somehow, irrationally, managed to make him feel guilty, and her words stung like salt in a wound. But Michael Bradford Winters was an expert at keeping his true feelings hidden. Instead, he just looked fierce, dark, and bristling with annoyance.

It was contagious. "Now what are *you* angry about, Michael?" she asked, riding the easy slide from sadness to anger.

"I am not angry," he insisted, eyes narrowed.

"Good thing too! I mean, I don't have to like everything you do. You certainly don't need my approval."

"No, I certainly don't."

"And you certainly didn't ask my opinion."

"No, I certainly didn't."

"And you certainly aren't going to change your mind."

"The deal is signed. I'd be a fool to reverse it."

"Fine. Then what are we arguing about?"

With his eyes he took in the measure of her spunk. A small smile tugged at the corner of his mouth. "I'm not sure," he admitted. "I'm not used to someone *dis*approving. That's twice in twenty-four hours you've been critical of my method of operation."

"And that doesn't happen often?"

He laughed. "That doesn't happen at all."

She slipped a conciliatory arm through his, resting her cheek against the hard curve of his shoulder. "See, you should have put me on that early plane. Or let me drown. Now you've got yourself your very own albatross!" She smiled up at him, feeling inexplicably and totally connected to him.

He bent his dark head, searching her eyes. There was no coyness there, just a thread of connection, an unexpected intimacy he had never found before, not anywhere, not with anyone. It scared the hell out of him.

Leaning away, he still held tight to her arm. "Do you want to see something beautiful?" he asked.

"If you promise not to sell it."

"No." He grinned at her, a reckless, Tom Sawyer kind of grin. "I'd like to *buy* it. Come on."

He took her farther around the pier, up and down the smooth wooden ramps and walkways, to a more isolated area. And there sat the most gorgeous yacht she could ever imagine.

"Oh, my," she said breathily. Her eyes were filled

with the gleaming pristine whiteness of the vessel that lay before them.

"My sentiments exactly," Michael whispered. "Isn't she one of the most beautiful ships in the world?"

"Absolutely." She had now seen a total of two ships up close in her lifetime, but she was sure Michael was right.

"I'd give anything to own her."

As if on cue, one of the dark-suited bodyguards walked down the gangway and strode directly over to Michael.

"Mr. Winters, a letter for you."

Michael held the envelope in his hand for a second, one dark brow lifted in surprise, then read the letter.

A small smile appeared on his lips, then rose to his eyes. He nodded once, then again, and drew a pen out of his inside jacket pocket. He wrote a response on the bottom of the letter, folded it back into the envelope, and handed it to the bodyguard. "Would you take this back to Sheikh Hamoudi, please, with my thanks."

"What was that all about?" Cathy demanded, sensing his excitement.

"The sheikh has to fly home unexpectedly. He knows I admired *The Oracle*—this yacht." He nodded toward the sleek, shining ship. "And he wondered if I would like to try her out for a few days, with the possibility of purchase if I'm completely satisfied." His grin was wide as the ocean. "Do you approve of *that* offer, Ms. Stephenson?"

"Doesn't sound like you have anything to lose, Mr. Winters." She smiled back. "I'd say go for it."

Impulsively he grabbed her hands and pulled her up against his chest. "Come with me," he said softly.

"What?" She laughed, shaking her head at his madness. "Do you realize the soul searching and mental struggle I went through simply to agree to a later plane?"

"Yes. I know I'm lucky you stayed," he answered with sudden seriousness, his eyes plumbing the depth of her soul.

"I—I didn't mean it that way, Michael. No, I'm the lucky one. I loved every minute of today," she whispered, then playfully cocked her head to one side. "Well, *almost* every minute, but the good definitely outweighed the bad." She reached up and touched his face, the warmth of his skin branding her palm forever. "But now I'd better get back and find a job. I need to wake up from this fairy tale and face the real world. There's a hearth to sweep—"

"Pardon?" he asked, puzzled.

"It was a joke."

"But I'm serious, Cathy. Come with me. It will be just the two of us, and a small crew. You said it yourself: what's there to lose? Please, come with me." He took hold of her shoulders, holding her at arm's length in a grip that was gentle yet unyielding. "I'll give you an interview, some story you can sell when you get back to Orlando. And I need someone to take notes, handle correspondence, someone I can trust, someone who'll be honest with me." He smiled at her. "Who else could I find to fit that bill on such short notice? It'll be only a few days. And the pay is good. Guaranteed. You'll make enough to let you look for a job later with ease."

"We're both a little crazy, Mr. Winters." Cathy took a deep breath and looked out over the ocean, the blue, deep, unknown, and unexplored ocean, and smiled a secret little smile. "Well, okay, I'll do it! One last adventure. And then Cinderella needs to collect herself and go back to more normal means of transportation."

"Cinderella, I like that." Michael's fingers brushed the soft skin on her neck. "Does that make me the prince?"

"Just for today," she said.

"And what a fine pumpkin we have waiting for us."

"A fine pumpkin, indeed." Cathy nodded, the sunlight shining warm on the top of her head. She could almost feel her feet leaving the ground, her body and soul rising higher and higher into some only-imagined fairyland. She almost hated to speak, to chance shattering the mood. Finally she tilted her head back and looked up at him. "When? When would we leave?"

"Now," Michael said, "I think now will be just fine."

Six

Once Gap had bought a car without careful thought. She had simply walked into Herb Allen's place on Third Street with her bills stuffed in her purse, and walked out with a 1957 Chevy. It was the most spontaneous thing ever done in the history of the Stephenson family and was faithfully committed to memory by every living relative so the story could be retold at family gatherings, and thereby be assured its rightful place in history.

But this . . . this yacht-borrowing, island-selling stuff was something else, and although she was trying to be composed, Cathy was having trouble dealing with it. She looked out over the magnificent expanse of brilliant green water and tried to shake away the fuzziness of unreality. It was really happening, it *was*. It wasn't an old Cary Grant movie or a wild dream. It was real.

It had been ninety minutes since the steward had

relayed the sheikh's offer to Michael, and in that amount of time, the same amount it usually took Cathy to clean out her closet, they had boarded a boat, left the picture-perfect cays behind, and were moving out into open water. The yacht had a crew, a chef, staterooms with flowers and baskets of fruit, closets filled with clothes.

And Cathy and Michael.

Cathy and Michael!

Cathy sighed and gripped the polished railing.

When Michael had excused himself earlier and gone to check on beam lengths, draft, and cruising range—terms as unfamiliar to Cathy as those in astrophysics—she had been almost relieved. It was so difficult to think with him at her side, so difficult to process all the things happening to her.

"How will I ever readjust to my ordinary life?" Cathy asked a passing sea gull.

The gull, his wings flashing silver in the brilliant blue sky, did not offer an answer; he simply soared on over the water, dipping down now and then to tease a fish and hunt for dinner.

Cathy grinned at the bird's antics. It so perfectly entertained her that she was tempted to think the gulls had been specially trained to follow the yacht around and perform on cue. It would certainly fit into this whole crazy world in which she was cavorting.

"Do you need for anything, ma'am?"

Cathy looked up into the serious brown face of a steward.

"Need?" she echoed. "I have more at my fingertips than anyone could *possibly* need. Look at this!" She pointed out across the water at the sunstreaked waves and colorful sailboats. "This is a paradise, more than any one person might have or see in a lifetime."

"Ma'am?" The young man's face contorted into a giant question mark. "English not so good," he finally managed to explain.

"It's okay," she said, charming him with a brilliant smile until his face relaxed. "I don't need anything. I'm fine, everything's fine," she assured him. And then, before she could confuse him further, she walked down to the yacht's elegant salon.

It was at the far end of the ship, a room suffused with golden light and filled with soft leather sofas inviting her to sit and relax and forget about worries.

"A drink, Ms. Stephenson?"

Cathy jumped. The steward stood smiling over her. "Diet Coke?" she asked, regaining her bearings.

He was back in a minute, carefully placed a lead crystal glass on the coffee table, and then on silent cushioned soles, he disappeared.

Cathy curled herself up into the corner of the sofa. The enormous vase of fresh flowers on the coffee table filled the room with the delicious fragrance of the cays. She drew a deep comforting breath, counted to five, and then picked up the top magazine from the pile the sheikh had left behind. Her heart thudded to a stop.

There he was, as big as life, looking up at her. It was Michael Winters, The Great American Bachelor, giving the camera a relaxed stare, his own eyes unreadable, his thoughts hidden. But in the careless pose was enough energy to warm half of America's female population. Cathy shivered. She had glanced at the article on the flight down to Orlando, when

Michael was as remote and unknown to her as the Pope. And now . . .

Quickly she turned the pages to the lengthy article that detailed Michael's financial successes and handball scores with equal attention.

She scanned the pages to refresh her memory, but now that she knew him, she realized just how little he had been willing to reveal. There were the obligatory facts: born in Massachusetts, graduated second in his class from Harvard Business School and headed WINTEX, a New York–based international real estate development empire worth a hundred million or so. And that was it.

Nothing to sneeze at! Cathy grinned, but where was the real Michael?

Oh, she could just imagine the frustrated reporter who had pried and prodded and come up empty. Michael had given them the portrait required: the elusive, successful bachelor . . . but nothing else.

The magazine slipped to her lap. Resting her head against the back of the couch, she closed her eyes. Truth be told, she didn't really know Michael either, so who was she to pass judgment? But already she knew far more than the article said. She knew about the kindness behind his mesmerizing glance; she knew about a laugh that was deep and rich and not used nearly often enough; yes, and she knew about a man who would risk his life to save an Indiana nobody; she knew about that broad, tanned chest and the warm feel of his flesh, the taste of his mouth. . . .

Cathy sighed and her breathing became slower and deeper. She felt light and dreamy. Yes, ordinary ol' Cathy Stephenson knew more about The Great American Bachelor than millions of readers nationwide. Wasn't that amazing? Huge Technicolor images flashed behind her closed eyelids: porpoises and yachts and sports cars and the wide blue sea. There was Cathy, tossed on top of a majestic wave, and there was Michael, waiting to catch her in one glorious movement of his muscled arms. . . .

Michael stood at the door of the salon and watched Cathy sleep.

Funny, he had been away from her for less than an hour and yet he had somehow felt the time, felt the length of her absence.

Fading sunlight cast lazy shadows across her face and he was drawn closer. In sleep she lost her effervescent sparkle, but something else, something equally lovely and heartstopping, had taken its place. It was a kind of peace, a repose that was totally foreign to Michael. Repose was something you achieved when you died, he had always thought. Yet on Cathy's innocent face it was magical, something coveted, something he knew he could make a million on if he could put it on the New York Stock Exchange. He shoved his hands into the pockets of his white pants and walked across the thick carpeting to where she slept.

The magazine was still there, opened to the last page of an article and balanced on the curve of her legs. Michael picked it up.

Cathy shifted slightly on the couch but did not awaken, not even when Michael sat down at the edge of the cushion. He watched her for a few minutes longer, then glanced at the article.

Damn, of all the things she could be reading, why this? What could she possibly think it had to tell her? It was nonsense, one of those image enhancers that seemed to be a required part of his life. He couldn't even remember agreeing to it in the first place. Most likely it was the result of careful maneuvering by his business advisers, something they thought would contribute to the bounty. The bachelor stuff was simply a fact, but for reasons beyond his comprehension, the media found that fascinating. He still found it odd that the topic could merit time on talk shows and expensive space in a magazine, when to him it was far more intriguing that people chose *to* marry.

Now, there was the mystery! To Michael's highly tuned, analytical mind, there was no good reason for getting married. Not if one weighed possible loss versus possible gain. Not if one relied on statistics. Not if he were to judge by his own past experiences with women on how many continents? None of it added up to a good reason to get married. And he was an expert at knowing when to be wary, if the venture was to be worthwhile.

Then he glanced back at Cathy.

Michael swallowed hard.

What was going on here? The last thing he needed was complications, especially with an uncomplicated, vulnerable young woman. He did not want a relationship. He did not even want an affair, dammit. He did not have the time. Company in bed was good enough, especially when the woman was as busy and preoccupied as he was. He liked conversation that went: "Good view. Good body. Good time. Good-bye." What did he know from grandmothers named Gap and rocking chairs and apple pies and shelling walnuts and working your way *up* to assistant editor in Orlando, Florida? And then there were puppies, kittens, kids, bottles and PTAs and . . .

Damn, he knew he needed a scotch when all that was starting to sound good just because of the way a woman looked asleep on a couch, her lips parted, lashes resting on her flushed cheeks. And besides, her hair was too curly!

Scowling, he stalked silently outside, signaled a drink from a steward, and stationed himself at the rail, hoping for a good storm to take his mind off his desire.

When Cathy found him standing there an hour later, his shirt and face wet from the relentless cold spray of the ocean, the embers were only beginning to cool.

"Hi!" she said. "Gorgeous evening, isn't it?"

She looked radiant, refreshed by her nap, relaxed, and totally at ease with herself.

Michael wanted to jump overboard—or throw her down on the deck right then and there. He gripped the rail so hard his knuckles showed white. "Lovely evening," he agreed with a groan.

"Anything wrong?" The breeze lifted her curls into a fuzzy brown halo.

"Not a thing."

Cathy shrugged. There was no understanding this man. He had everything in the world, and yet he always seemed uptight and irritable. "So, what's on for tonight?"

Again a groan gathered in his throat. Michael clenched his jaw, closed his eyes, and gripped the rail. Then, without looking at her, he shrugged. "Whatever you like. There's a private screening room and an entire library of classic films. Or we could have a late dinner poolside and a swim. Or"—he wiped his brow—"we could gamble a bit. There's a small casino, Vegas rules, a few slots . . . we'd have it all to ourselves. You do gamble?"

"Bingo at the VFW," she admitted with a shrug of her narrow shoulders.

From the look of pain that flashed across his handsome face, she could tell it was somehow the answer he had feared.

"Sorry." She offered a little laugh of apology.

"No problem," he said. "How about this? Shall we dress for dinner, formal"—he decided wisely the more clothes between them the better off he'd be—"and I'll teach you a little blackjack and roulette?" A large, well-lit room sounded far more prudent than a moonwashed deck!

"Sounds great!"

Her eyes sparkled like stars, like flecks of gold dust in a miner's hands. A treasure. The real thing.

"Fine," he said quickly, some bizarre pain shooting through his chest. "I'm going to go work off this scotch in the exercise room. I'll knock on your cabin door about eight? Now, if you'll excuse me—"

And he was gone.

Cathy looked after him with a little smile. She had felt his desire, seen the line of sweat along his upper lip. And now she was feeling, well, more than a little flattered, and sort of pleased with herself.

After all, she had been raised in Indiana, not a convent!

And this was the stuff that fairy tales were made of!

Later that night, wearing an off-the-shoulder confection of apricot silk that she found hanging in her closet, they played blackjack in their own private casino. She beat him. Twice.

"Here you are," she said solemnly, counting chips into the palm of his hand. "Here's the twenty dollars you staked me to. And one more for interest . . . I insist! And now I'm on my own, right?" She pocketed the rest.

"You don't have to pay me back, Cathy." He laughed, leaning over her to catch another breath of her sweet smell of soap and perfume. "Maybe I want you in my debt."

" 'Neither a borrower nor a lender be,' " she quipped back, drunk on the elegance of the room and the desire in his eyes. "Now teach me to play roulette!" She slipped an arm through his and led him toward the roulette table.

Their reflection in the mirror made her pause. There they were, the handsomest man she'd ever seen, in a tuxedo and a white, starched, ruffled shirt, black satin bow tie, and cummerbund, tall and powerfully built, broad shoulders and lean hard hips . . . and a beautiful woman. With a toss of her head she gave a little laugh and squeezed his arm. "Michael, they would *not* believe this in Indiana!"

At first she didn't trust the roulette wheel.

"How do I know he spins that little ball the same way every time?" she said behind one hand, lifting one brow toward the stone-faced Arab behind the table.

"Why would he want to fix it?" Michael whispered back.

"Fix it?" she asked aloud.

"Never mind. Trust me. Put a chip on a lucky number, or the corner of two or four numbers, or out here—" He pointed as he explained the rules, the odds, the strategy. Then he folded his arms across his chest. "Okay, ready to bet?"

"What are you going to bet?" she asked softly, eyeing the wheel with increased mistrust.

"Fifty on nine. Fifty on thirty-six. Fifty on double zero."

"Okay." She nodded. "I'll put five on number . . . three." She plunked it down with great enthusiasm.

Nine won.

"Oh." She gave a sigh, nibbled at one corner of her mouth. "Okay, here's five on number eighteen, and . . . five on three. I like that number!"

She lost.

And lost.

And lost again.

"Let me loan you a few," Michael insisted, pushing a tall tower of chips toward her across the green felt.

"No." She shook her head, pushing them back. She fished her last two chips out of her jeweled evening bag and held them in her closed hand. Her heart was pounding. Her throat hurt. This was fun?

"Okay," she whispered, "one on eighteen, and one . . . on three."

Three won.

"What? Really? Oh, I knew it. That's Gap's birthday, May third! Oh, how much *is* that?" she crowed as the dealer pushed the stack of chips in front of her.

"Three hundred and fifty dollars."

"What? That's incredible! Is this for real, or do we have to pay him back at the end of the night?"

Michael gave a great shout of laughter. "No, dear one, it's for real."

"Then I want to cash it in. Right now! Hurry—"

"Why? Let's keep playing for a while—"

"And lose it? Never!"

"Then put yours away and play with my chips." He held out a handful.

"I couldn't," she said honestly. "It's a lot of money. I wouldn't feel comfortable."

Without waiting for him, she hurried over to the cashier's cage. When she came back, her face was flushed, her eyes shining. "Here I am. Now what?"

"You tell me," he answered, shoving his hands deep into his pockets. "Some people have been known to gamble into the wee hours of the morning; so far we have been here thirty minutes."

"Then let's! Though I can't figure out why you like it—*you* especially. For a man who likes everything well-planned and under control, this seems very chancy."

"It's called a calculated risk; it makes life exciting."

"Fine," she said, "go on and take the risk. You play, and I'll watch. I'll even blow on your dice, or whatever 'some people' do for luck." She winked.

"But I wanted *you* to enjoy yourself." He stood there stubbornly, his eyes dark and slightly annoyed.

Cathy had to laugh. *I shouldn't, I shouldn't . . .* she thought to herself, but she couldn't help it. Her amusement came bubbling out like warm, shaken soda pop. "You just don't like having your plans changed on you, Mr. Winters."

Michael placed both hands on his hips and leaned over her. "I beg your pardon."

"Come on!" She grinned, looping her arm tightly through one of his. "Come take me for a stroll on deck. I feel wonderful, and lucky and rich . . . and beautiful, and I want to be outside under a star-studded sky."

And suddenly all the emotions he had balanced on top of his desire tumbled like a house of cards, and he was left with this gut-wrenching, burning ache of passion. "Yes"—he grabbed her hand—"come on."

They climbed the stairway hand in hand. Michael held the door open and Cathy stepped past, her arm, shoulder, dress brushing against him. Through his clothes his skin burned. She walked to the rail, heels clicking on the teak deck, and he followed her, stood behind her, pushed his face into her hair.

"Michael! I thought we were strolling."

"Later. A little later." His breath slid down her scalp like fingers. "I want you."

"What?"

He swallowed hard. "I want you . . . to see the stars. I thought you wanted stars."

"Yes," she whispered, leaning her curly brown head back against his shoulder. "Tell me about them."

For the first time in his life Michael Winters could not come up with an easy reply. There was a knot of longing tying up his throat; his tongue was thick;

his chest hurt. Right there, the whole length of his chest and belly, he could feel the delicate knobs of her spine, the innocent thrust of her hips, the curve of her buttocks. She fit against him so perfectly, so sweetly, as if she were part of him, connected to him, a slim young branch grafted to the trunk of his tree.

"Cathy—" Her name, half whisper, half groan, gathered in his throat. He wrapped his arms around her, buried his face in her hair.

For Cathy, it was like being swept under by the sea again. One minute there were stars, sky, air to breathe—and the next she was turning in his arms, turning in the dark, turning to the sound of her name on his lips and the feel of his lips on her mouth, and the hard, hungry thrust of his tongue.

She did not fight. She threw her arms around his neck, pressed into his chest, opened her mouth, and met his tongue with her own, touching tip to tip, sliding, curling, darting like two fish in warm, sweet underwater caves. She drank in his kisses, nibbled on his lips, rubbed her mouth against his one way and another, their lips meeting and parting and meeting again. She pushed her hands through his dark thick hair, down his neck, over the broad span of his shoulders, while his hands dove up to the wrists into her springy brown curls.

His breath was her breath, his heartbeat hers. The soft, guttural gasps and animal sounds were torn from his throat, or hers. The heat burning between them rose from his body, or hers. "Michael, Michael," she breathed, hearing his name inside her head, against his lips, without knowing she'd spoken.

"Cathy—" His tongue traced a warm, wet trail down the hollow of her throat; his mouth hovered over her pulse; his breath flowed over her breasts like water. "Let's go down to my cabin."

Eyes closed tight, she rubbed her cheek against the top of his head, aroused to trembling by the brush of his hair against her face. Her knees were going. Her sanity was going. Her self-control was gone.

But not quite. Behind her closed eyes she saw a line. There was this thin, thin line, between wanting and wanting desperately; between desire and downright lust; between like and love. A little line, visible only to her, drawn right there between them, between Michael and her, and she was right at the edge. Even closer! One foot had even wiggled its way over, and she could feel the trembling climbing up from her toes, through her weak knees, through the marrow of her bones turned to water . . . right to her heart.

Tears stung behind her lids. Pushing him away, pulling herself away took all the strength she had. She forced a weak little laugh. "Michael—I thought you were going to show me the stars."

"I'm seeing stars," he said in a voice that was little more than a growl. He reeled back against the rail. His chest heaved with labored breaths; his arms hung empty. "Damn, woman . . . what happened?"

"Nothing happened," she answered quickly, striving vainly for levity. "And given the circumstances, that seems like the best idea."

"Not *my* idea," he groaned. Throwing his head back, he gulped in huge lungfuls of sobering salt air. "Cathy. Cathy. Cathy." He shook his head, eyes closed, mouth closing tight over the tiny syllables of her name. "Why not? Just tell me why not."

"Because this is a test run of the yacht, not us. There is no 'us.' I'm Cathy Stephenson from Indiana, remember, and I will soon be back in Orlando, looking for a job, paying the rent, making my once every two weeks phone call to Gap to tell her how nicely my life is running, how smoothly, how sanely. And you, if you've forgotten, are Michael Bradford Winters. The Great American Bachelor." She tipped her head to one side, folded her arms across her chest, and asked something she'd been wanting to ask all along. "Why, Michael? I mean, I can sort of understand; there must be a thousand women out there, all wanting to get just a taste of you, your money, your life . . . marriage not a prerequisite. But why "Great American"? Was that their label or yours?"

"I don't remember," he answered evasively. He leaned his elbows back on the rail and narrowed his eyes till his lids almost hid the blue.

"Let me rephrase that," she quipped. "Is that decision final?"

"About not marrying?"

She laughed. "No, I'm taking a poll on staunch Republicans and their commitment to defense spending."

"Funny, Stephenson."

"I aim to please."

"No, you don't," he countered, enjoying all this despite himself.

But suddenly she was serious. "Yes, I do, Michael.

But right now, at least for now, the one I have to please is me. My own sense of rightness. Of what's real . . . and what's only fantasy."

He looked at her so hard and long, he could have been memorizing her.

Cathy waited, then broke the silence. "You still haven't answered me, Michael."

"Because I don't know, not anymore. Not with you." He shook his head and breathed deeply. Then he looked at her again.

He noticed she was still trembling, despite the stubborn lift of her chin, despite the firmness of her determined little smile. He reached over and brushed the backs of his fingers against her cheek.

"Want to take that stroll now?"

She nodded, knowing if she opened her mouth to say a word, she'd beg him to hold her again, kiss her again, love her.

Cinderella really wanted the prince, even as she ran away down the steps to the carriage waiting to turn back into a pumpkin.

Oh, how was she ever going to live a pumpkin life again, after this night at the ball? But to have never met him, never kissed him, never felt what she was feeling? No. That was worse. Unthinkable. Somehow when the clock struck twelve or one or whatever hour at whatever dock or airport, she would smile and chalk it up to an adventure.

She tried the smile on for size just to make sure it still fit. There. Fine and dandy. Hunky-dory!

Drawing a deep breath, she sashayed off down the deck. "Well, are you coming? Look at that ocean, that sky! There's no telling where one starts and the

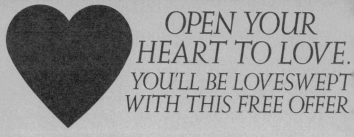

OPEN YOUR HEART TO LOVE.
YOU'LL BE LOVESWEPT WITH THIS FREE OFFER

HERE'S WHAT YOU GET:

1. **FREE! SIX NEW LOVESWEPT NOVELS!** You get 6 beautiful stories filled with passion, romance, laughter, and tears...exciting romances to stir the excitement of falling in love... again and again.

2. **FREE! A BEAUTIFUL MAKEUP CASE WITH A MIRROR THAT LIGHTS UP!** What could be more useful than a makeup case with a mirror that lights up*? Once you open the tortoise-shell finish case, you have a choice of brushes...for your lips, your eyes, and your blushing cheeks.

*(batteries not included)

3. **SAVE! MONEY-SAVING HOME DELIVERY!** Join the Loveswept at-home reader service and we'll send you 6 new novels each month. You always get 15 days to preview them before you decide. Each book is yours for only $2.09 — a savings of 41¢ per book.

4. **BEAT THE CROWDS!** You'll always receive your Loveswept books before they are available in bookstores. You'll be the first to thrill to these exciting new stories.

BE LOVESWEPT TODAY — JUST COMPLETE, DETACH AND MAIL YOUR FREE-OFFER CARD.

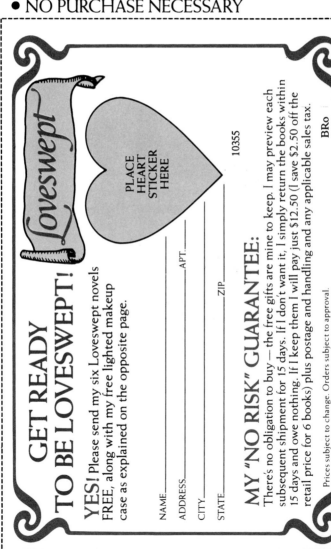

REMEMBER!

- The free books and gift are mine to keep!
- There is no obligation!
- I may preview each shipment for 15 days!
- I can cancel anytime!

other ends. I mean, how do you know which way the boat's going?"

"Ship," he corrected her automatically, striding up to her and matching his pace and tone to hers. "And you watch the water, there, just below us. See how it curls out and back? We're going this way—" He pointed out into the velvet darkness, his other hand resting casually on her arm. "East southeast. During the night we'll pass Eleuthera and then tomorrow we'll sail past Cat Island, maybe anchor for a while between Rum Cay and Watling Island, and swing out across the Tropic of Cancer heading for the Turks and Caicos."

"That's all out there?" She was dazzled by the wonder of it all, hidden in the dark, just over the horizon.

Michael tightened his grip on the rail. "I'm beginning to think there's a lot out there we don't expect until we sail right into it." His voice was low, the words meant only for himself. And they were blown away by the breeze and the spray.

But the woman at his side felt his gaze, and trembled.

How were they ever going to get through the next few days?

Seven

"Gap always told me not to put anything in my mouth if I didn't know where it had been," Cathy said, backing away from the snorkeling equipment Michael held in his outstretched hand.

"Come on, Cathy—"

"No way, Michael! One underwater adventure will last me a lifetime."

"But this isn't underwater; you just float on the surface—"

"*You* float on the surface. I'd sink like a stone, like an Indiana rock! No way. Go if you want."

"Would I let anything happen to you?" he teased, his eyes as changeable and clear as the blue sea around them.

"If it meant getting your way, Mr. Winters, you're capable of anything. Having spent three solid days with you, I'd swear to that in court."

"I don't think that's a very flattering assessment."

He grinned, cocking both hands on his hips, the snorkeling mask and tube resting against his long, solid, very tanned thigh.

"I didn't know you wanted to be flattered." She kept her eyes on his, knowing how susceptible she was to persuasion by that gorgeous but not-yet-familiar body. "You're wasting your time, Michael."

"You'd make me go alone? Knowing it isn't safe?"

"And just what good would I be?"

He stepped closer. "You'd throw yourself between me and danger," he whispered. "You'd give me mouth-to-mouth resuscitation."

Suddenly her mouth was too dry to speak, her knees too weak to stand. She wobbled to the nearest chair.

"Michael, don't make me do this."

"Hey, I'm just fooling around." He sank to his knees in front of her, mistaking her arousal for honest fear. "We won't go if you don't want to. That's it."

Crazy, crazy, crazy. His nearness only made things worse. Kneeling in front of her, an inch from her knees, she could smell the clean, salt-sprayed, delicious smell of his body. Could feel the heat radiating from him. Could reach out and push back the dark, thick, windblown hair on his forehead.

Slipping sideways off the chair, she went to fiddle with some papers on a desk. "Let me think about it, okay?" She slid him a quick glance. "Is it really nice?"

"It's beautiful. Safe. Easy. If you can shower you can snorkel," he assured her. "We could even hold hands. And the water's warm as a bath, and clear, and you can see the coral and the fish—"

She was not listening. Inside her head she was watching a movie: Michael and Cathy, holding hands, gliding silently through crystal-clear waters, the same sea washing over them both, touching them from head to toe, flowing over shoulders, chests, hips, thighs . . .

This was getting obsessive!

Cut it out, Stephenson! she ordered herself silently, and her head flicked off the film. But her body was on its own, loose, wet . . .

Out loud she said, "I should be earning my keep. Let me send that fax through to New York for you, and we'll talk about this later."

"Can't. Bridge says the machine's down, that and the radio. I think that's why they were so eager to have us off the ship. They must be afraid I'll go crazy without access to world markets!" He laughed.

"Astute crew!"

"Very funny, Cathy." He frowned, the corners of his eyes crinkling. "I haven't been that bad, have I?"

"No, but 'business is business.' " She tossed back his motto in a little singsong chant, then winked. "Actually you seem quite relaxed for a very uptight, stressed-out entrepreneurial type."

"They say snorkeling is the best cure for that." He moved close again, pressing his advantage.

All the oxygen seemed to vanish from the room. She could not breathe, let alone fight. "Let's give it a try." She nodded and hurried out on deck.

"Good afternoon, Ms. Stephenson." Blocking her path was an Arab speaking perfectly polished English. "Have you and Mr. Winters decided to try the snorkeling, or perhaps take a small boat over to one of the cays?"

"Exactly what we just decided." Cathy gulped, nodding again. She stepped around him to the rail. "You'll have to speak to Mr. Winters about the details."

The details took less than thirty minutes.

With a splash, the crew lowered an eight-foot rubber dinghy loaded with snorkeling gear, paddles, a large picnic chest, a duffel bag with a change of clothes for each of them, straw hats, suntan lotion, towels, a blanket, a jug of fresh water, a map, first aid kit, and safety flares.

"Goodness! You'd think we were going for a week!" Cathy laughed.

"They certainly are well trained. I guess the sheikh and his friends don't travel light," Michael agreed with a shake of his dark head. "Well, let's get going. Here, hold my hand and just climb on down the rope ladder."

"You go first!" Cathy insisted.

"Okay, here we go. Think of it as an adventure."

Cathy took a deep breath and descended the ladder after him, pretending that her heart was *not* pounding, her pulse *not* racing. "So what now?"

"We're off." He grinned, and waved up to the crew on the deck above. "I think we've got everything. Thank you! See you late this afternoon."

"Whatever you say," drifted down the reply.

• • •

Using the bright yellow paddles, Michael rowed them toward the nearest cays. The water shimmered in the sun, changing from blue to turquoise to azure, then pale green. From her seat in the raft, Cathy watched the bright, flitting shapes of fish. She leaned over and dangled her fingers in the water. It *was* warm as a bath, clear and sparkling, and with the tropical sunshine beating on her head and shoulders, she was eager to jump in.

"I think I'm going to like this, Mr. Winters." She smiled. She flicked a handful of water at his bare chest and laughed when he jumped.

"Hey, no fair!"

"Who said I had to be fair?" She giggled, sprinkling him again.

"You asked for it!" He made a quick move with one paddle, and soaked her head to foot.

"You'll pay for that!" she sputtered, water running into her eyes. "Just you wait!"

"I've been waiting for days," he said almost solemnly.

"Hmph!" She folded her arms over her wet chest and bit back a laugh. "Hey, look at that!" She pointed, her attention suddenly caught by a dark ridge just under the water. "What's that?"

"Coral reef," Michael explained, lifting the oar and letting the raft glide on. "Beautiful, isn't it? Great spot for snorkeling. Here, let's row into the lagoon just a little farther, and I'll get us all set up here. You'll love it. You'll see fish you've never imagined, all colors and shapes, and the coral itself is beautiful. Though it looks tough, it's really very vulnerable, but there are a few things to be wary of." He stowed the oars as he talked, gently lowered a small anchor, sorted out their gear.

After he fit the snorkeling tube onto his mask, he instructed, "Now, you lower the mask like this, then put the mouthpiece in your mouth, bite down here, and close your lips tight like this."

Cathy wanted to fall over backward laughing! She struggled to keep a straight face.

"What's so funny?" he demanded, one dark brow lifted.

"You! Always so perfect, so polished . . . and here you are looking like the creature from the Black Lagoon."

"This is not a beauty contest—"

"Lucky for you!" She cut him off with another burst of laughter. "I've got to tell you, you would have saved the women of America a lot of heartache if they had put *this* picture on the cover of *Time*.

"That would have suited me fine! Now, could you please try to be serious?" he demanded, fighting hard not to laugh with her.

"No."

He splashed her with a maskful of water, laughing so hard the raft rocked.

She splashed him back.

Across the water came the unexpected sound of a motor, an outboard revved to maximum speed. The noise turned their heads around, and Michael shaded his eyes against the sun, peering into the distance toward the yacht.

"What the—?"

"Who's that?" Cathy asked, squinting into the sun.

"I don't know. It looks like the crew's lifeboat from the yacht."

He stood up, legs spread for balance, making the raft rock gently. "It is! And it's full; they must all be on it. What the hell—?"

The small boat raced out of sight. The sound faded. The sea was silent again.

And then, while Michael and Cathy rocked on the lovely clear waters and watched in utter disbelief, the yacht blew up.

Boom! It seemed to lift off the water and come back down in Tinkertoy pieces. Gone.

Cathy sat with her mouth open, clinging to the rocking sides of the rubber raft. "Oh . . ." she gasped. "Oh, Michael! Oh . . ."

"Oh, damn!" Michael finished her sentence. He folded his arms across his chest and sat staring out at the water.

"It blew up," Cathy whispered, unbelieving.

"Someone blew it up," Michael corrected her. "At least they were polite enough to get us off first."

"But why?" Cathy breathed, looking around over her shoulders as if expecting to find an assassin lurking there. She wrapped her arms around herself to stop the shaking.

"Probably something to do with oil prices, dollars per barrel, barrels per day. The sheikh's been right in the middle of the battle to hold oil prices steady. This was probably someone registering their displeasure with his last OPEC vote. Probably just—"

"—just 'business'?" Cathy finished for him this time.

"Just business," he agreed, his voice flat. "Nothing personal."

"But what do we do now?" she whispered.

Michael sat silently for a minute, weighing their options, his gaze scanning the sea. When he looked back at Cathy, his face was calm and his voice was deep and soothing, but his eyes were dark with the promise of adventure.

"There are sure to be rescue planes. A search party. But for now, how about a clambake on the beach, Indiana?"

Eight

Michael set off one flare on the beach. Then, avoiding Cathy's look of dismay, he shut the box on the rest. "Help couldn't get here this quickly; we'd better save the others."

It was almost the truth. He knew, judging by how far they had sailed and how few of these tiny cays were inhabited, that rescue *was* unlikely this soon. But the whole truth was, Michael wasn't sure he wanted to be rescued. At least not yet.

Dripping wet, the sun beating on his head and shoulders, everything they owned scattered over the sand, Michael Winters felt better than he had in years. Better than better. He felt great! And why shouldn't he? Here he was, stranded on a tropical island with a beautiful woman he had been lusting after for days . . . plenty of food and water . . . even dry clothes and a blanket. *Paradise.*

A twinge of guilt marred his contentment when he glanced at Cathy.

She caught his eye and stepped close to where he was kneeling, resting a hand on his shoulder. "How long do you think it will take?" she asked, her teeth chattering.

"Not long." He stood and pulled her close. "But don't worry. We're safe. We have plenty of supplies. And I'm here to protect you."

She gave him a faint smile, making him feel guiltier than ever.

"Why don't you get out of that wet suit?" he said quickly, and rooted around in the duffel bag until he came up with a pair of shorts, a T-shirt, and even a lacy little bra and panties. "That's what I call being prepared; the boy scouts would be proud of us! Here, you'll feel better when you're warm and dry."

"Where should I change?" She held the bundle to her chest.

"Right here is fine." He pretended to look around. "I'd say this is fairly private."

Not private enough, she thought. She headed up the beach toward the palms and palmettos. "You wait there," she called over her shoulder. "But keep your ears open; get ready to come if I yell for help." The thought of snakes had crossed her mind.

In two seconds she was dressed and heading back down at a run, her wet suit swinging from one hand by its shoulder straps. "I'm back! I'm fine." She gasped, laughing at herself.

"And I'm very glad to see you." Michael's matching laughter turned to a husky groan as he buried his face in her wet hair. "Don't worry, Cathy. Everything will be fine. This will be great, you'll see. An adventure!"

She almost believed him. At least she tried, following his lead as he sorted through the supplies, stowed them safely away from the surf, spread their suits out to dry, one next to the other. It all looked as ordinary as Gap's Monday-morning wash.

As night fell, she was tired, scared, and miserable. She wanted a bed to lie on, with walls around it, and a roof over her head, and either a house or a boat—correction, a ship—just *something* solid.

Instead, she had a deserted island.

True, she also had Michael Winters, the Great American Bachelor, alone on that island, but each time she began to relax and contemplate the pleasure of that fact, she heard a noise among the trees.

"What was that?" she yelped, the hair on her neck and arms prickling.

"Hmmm?" Michael was busy checking the contents of the first aid kit.

"Michael, did you hear that noise?" She stood so close she stepped on his toes.

"What noise?" he asked, slipping a reassuring arm around her waist.

They listened, but there was only silence. The wind had died, and the waves slapped lazily at the sand.

"Well, I heard it!" she insisted. "It sounded like some kind of animal—"

"Probably a lizard. They're all over the tropics."

She immediately pictured something huge and scaled, a darting tongue, beady eyes. "I hate lizards," she announced, hugging her elbows with both hands.

"They're tiny, and certainly more frightened of you than you are of them." He did not even glance up.

She shrugged, sighed, and wandered down toward the water.

In seconds she came running back, lifting her feet high off the ground with every step. "Michael, help! Ow! Oh, Michael. *Ow!* Oh, something's biting my feet!" She was hopping from one foot to the other, grimacing at each tiny red-hot stab of pain. "Ow! Michael, help me!"

"Sand flies," he answered calmly, using his wet shirt to rub her ankles.

"That's not doing a damn bit of good!" she answered ungratefully. "*Do* something!"

He looked down at her, his eyes dark with amusement, half boy scout, half devil. "What would you like me to do, Indiana?"

"Save me!"

"Okay." Without another word he picked her up and tossed her over his shoulder so that she was upside down, silenced by sheer surprise, clinging to him as he strode off up the beach. The blood rushed to her head. She grabbed on to the waistband of his trunks and held tight, her face pressed against the hard, smooth wall of his back, feeling his muscles working against her cheek as he loped along for a good quarter mile and rounded the point leading to narrow, surf-tossed beach.

"There." he knelt and laid her down upon the sand. "Better?"

She thought about it for a second. True, her feet were not being bitten to pieces, but she was dizzy, her ears hummed, and he was awfully close. So close she could smell the saltwater and sweat on him. And his knee was pressing right there between her thighs, his skin hot and raspy with sand.

"I'm not sure—" she murmured.

His eyes slid down over her face and her body, half hidden in the dusk. "Maybe I'd better check your pulse," he whispered, and pressed his lips to the hollow of her throat.

She closed her eyes.

He kissed her chin, the corner of her mouth, her ear, her eyelids. Then, as quickly as those delicious kisses started, they stopped.

Cathy took a deep breath and opened her eyes. Michael was staring down at her, his eyes all hot and hungry, blue as the center of a flame, hot and burning.

"Cathy—"

No man had ever looked at her like that before. No, she had never known a man who had that passion lurking behind his eyes, that flame burning. She knew if she let it, it would burn her to ashes and she would blow away on the wind.

She scrambled out from under him, stood, and tugged at the bottom of her shorts. "Thanks. How'd you do that?"

Crouched on the sand, he glared at her. "I didn't get a chance to *do* anything, Cathy."

She blushed. "I meant saving me from the sand flies; how'd you do that?"

He stood up, brushing sand off his calves and thighs. When he lifted his face, his eyes were a cool ice-blue. "No problem; you just have to know where the trade winds blow. Most things are easy once you understand what makes them work."

Cathy blushed again, caught on the point of the barb.

But at the same time, her temper rose. She did not want to be *easy*, as he so neatly put it. She did not want to be an anecdote in the latest tale he told his friends around some fancy table in Manhattan. But she was having a very hard time resisting him.

Her nice, safe life was falling away like the clothes on her back. Just the skimpiest bit was left to remind her of ordinariness and safety. And every day, every minute, it was getting harder to stay carefully on her side of the line.

"So, what now, Michael?" she asked, her voice low and trembly in the growing dark.

He looked at her for a long minute, knowing exactly what she was thinking, and knocked for a loop by the realization. *This was ridiculous!* In business he always had a sixth sense about what an opponent was thinking or planning, and he used it to his own advantage. He played the rest of his life by the same rules.

But this was different. *Cathy* was different. He had the oddest feeling deep in his gut, something that made him feel strangely protective and tender. His hand reached out to her and he saw how her cheek pinked as his fingers brushed her skin, how his own hand shook. His heart was slamming against his ribs, and when he spoke, his voice sounded full of sand.

"Wait here. I'll go fetch the stuff and build us a

fire, and I won't let anything hurt you, okay, Indiana? Okay?"

What could she do? That sudden tenderness of his brought her feelings back with a rush. "Okay." She smiled back. "Whatever you say."

And when he came back and built a fire, she nestled against him, trying to think of clever, endearing, charming things to say . . . but instead she fell sound asleep.

Michael never closed his eyes. And he never felt tired.

What the hell's going on, he wondered, and sat there all night, holding her close. He had a feeling the answer was like a tiny seed, hidden inside, just waiting for a little sunlight and rain.

Nine

Morning came earlier than it did in Indiana. Or Manhattan.

The sun sent pink and golden messengers streaming across the eastern sky, then pushed its way up over the horizon like some impatient royal visitor. It made the whole world sit up and take notice.

Birds sang and screeched and whistled. Sand crabs scuttled in and out of the surf. Lizards ran races along the palmetto leaves, flashing brown and green and vanishing into perfect camouflage. The pelicans came for breakfast, diving into the breakers, then throwing back their long, ugly heads and gulping fish.

Cathy loved the pelicans. Stout and grayish-brown, they did their crazy dives and then bobbed awkwardly on the waves. But when they flew, they all flew together, in formation, like good, careful friends, each one watching out for the other.

"Look at them, Michael." Cathy had her head tipped back, one hand thrown up to shield her eyes. "They're so beautiful."

Again he felt his heart knock around like a marble in a box. The sight of her was doing strange things to him. His concentration was shot to hell. He had counted their remaining supply of flares twice and still was not sure how many they had. He had dived into the surf three times already to cool down and found it wasn't the sun giving him trouble. Damn. He let out a harsh breath and rested his hands on his thighs, head down between his shoulders.

The touch of her small hand on his upper arm made him jump.

"You okay?" she asked, her brown eyes deep and sweet as chocolate.

"Fine," he answered. "We'd better get this stuff loaded in the dinghy and head on while the weather holds, okay?"

"Aye-aye, sir." She flipped him a little salute and bent to lift the cooler into the raft.

Her shorts hitched up and he could see how pink her thighs had gotten from all the sun yesterday, and the color on her shoulders and the back of her neck; even her nose was pink. It made him crazy.

A groan rose in his throat.

"Michael?"

"I'm fine."

"Are you sure?" She stepped closer and laid her palm against his forehead, her brow furrowed with worry, her breath sweet against his lips.

That did it. He grabbed her tight and kissed her, his mouth opening over hers as if he would swallow her, he was so hungry for the taste of her. The muscles along his arms ached, needing to curve around her, needing it as if they were made to hold her and not holding her was pain. The way his skin needed to feel her skin, his bones needed to match themselves to her bones, the whole slim length of her belonging there against the length of him.

"Whoa!" Cathy laughed then, struggling to slip her hands against his chest and catch her breath. "Michael, I thought you were the one who said we'd better get rolling." She was smiling, questioning, laughing, and aching all at the same time. But her eyes still said no.

"Hey, just a little early morning pick-me-up when there's no fresh o.j. nearby," he tossed back, grinning loose and easy as if he meant it. "Here, throw me those jugs of water, and the first aid kit, and we're ready to go. Off in search of civilization, right?"

"You betcha!"

He pulled the raft down just to the edge of the water, got her settled safely in the back, and then got into the front, already paddling. "You okay back there?"

"Fine and dandy."

"Now, we'll be all right until we hit the breakers. Then hold on tight and I'll get us through. After that it's just a matter of paddling."

"I can help," she offered, her words changing into a shriek as the first set of breakers tossed them up and sideways.

It was a good thing Michael was strong. Each crest threatened to toss them over, toss them back on the beach, but he fought through, the muscles roping on his shoulders and arms, his back glistening with sweat and sea spray. Then they were over into the open sea, where the water smoothed out into a tightly pulled sheet of blue.

"Wow!" Cathy gasped, laughing. "That was wild!"

"Glad you liked it." Michael laughed back, glad for the release that came with physical exertion. He could handle this. He could handle anything, always had, always would.

He paddled all morning, heading south, keeping the ocean on his left and the string of cays on his right. They were all uninhabited, mostly tiny, thick with tropical plants and palms, separated one from the other by a shallow green sea. By mid-morning he was starving, and he let Cathy take the oars while he downed a sandwich and a few carefully measured sips of fresh water.

When he took the oars back he saw how sunburnt her cheeks were. "Put that hat on, Cathy. And see if I put the suntan lotion in the first aid kit."

"Sunblock," she called back, holding up the tube. "Want some?"

"No, I'm fine. Just put it on your face and lips. And your eyelids too. Then keep the hat pulled low."

"Aye-aye, sir," she said.

Michael turned and caught her grinning, and he felt that now-familiar thud in his chest. "Just keep on following orders, matey," he joked back, then leaned into the oars with all his might.

Just after noon they saw a large cay, a small fishing boat, and a dock.

Cathy got so excited, she forgot to hold on. "Michael, look! People! A house! Civilization!"

"Hold on," he yelled back, trying to keep the raft steady.

"Sorry." She giggled, and settled down, but what she had started, the ocean made worse. The long swells rolling in toward shore seemed to rise and fall beneath them like a roller coaster. The little raft leapt and jumped, twisting sideways as the waves dropped out from under it.

"Hold on, Cathy," Michael yelled, all business now, grim and serious. "Just hold on. And watch out for the cooler; don't let it hit you if we go over."

"Go over?" Cathy repeated, grabbing hold of the raft's sides with shaking fingers.

"Just hang on—"

There was no hanging on. The reef below the water's surface churned the ocean into whitecaps. The little rubber raft jumped and dipped, jumped again, then flipped completely over.

Cathy took that familiar, horrifying plunge into deep water. And panicked.

But Michael was right there beside her before the salt could sting her throat. Ignoring the coral, the lost gear, the sinking raft, he went straight for Cathy, caught her tight against him, and pulled her over the reef and into the calm waters of the lagoon.

"You're okay," he whispered, brushing water and wet hair off her face with both hands.

"You bet," she said shakily. "Hey, I wasn't even worried."

"You didn't look worried," he lied back. Grinning, he dropped an arm over her slim shoulders and headed them toward shore.

Three men were on the dock, waving. The tallest,

a brown, spare old man in a fisherman's hat, called out to them, pointing up around the curve of the cay as he talked. "You see there, mistah? Up yonder? Dot's de way into harbor here. Not down here, no sir."

"Sorry we didn't know that sooner," Michael answered with a shrug of his broad shoulders. "I've never been here before, and we've got no maps or charts."

"Don't think we're on de maps," the man answered seriously. "But you're not the first. Over where you went down, a dinghy just like that one turn right over and everybody got lost. Two mens and one woman. Just about this time last year, yes."

"Oh, that's horrible," Cathy whispered, her hand pressed to her mouth.

"Oh, dat's not all. One time a boatful of ministers went down, right over dere, and only one swam to shore. Never did see hat or shoes of de others. Sharks run off with dem."

Cathy's eyes were wide as saucers.

"Enough." Michael tugged her close, jumped up onto the dock and lifted her up next to him. "Enough tales of woe for one day," he said sternly. "Let's go find the town and make some plans, okay?"

"Town's down de road a ways," the old man said, pointing off in the general direction. "Ask for Gloria when you gets there. She be glad to help."

A short while later, their feet, hair, and throats dusty, they found the dozen or so small buildings that made up the town. Gloria was behind the counter of the little grocery store.

Michael popped the tab off a beer and downed it

in almost one gulp. He sighed when he finished, then wiped his chin with the back of one hand. "Want one, Cathy?"

"What I really want is a nice warm shower. I feel like my skin is two parts dried salt, one part dust. And my hair—" Cathy pulled at her tangle of curls with both hands, and they sprang back, stiff and salty.

"If a shower's what you want, dere's one out back," Gloria offered. "First I make you a nice lime punch to take de thirst off, yes?"

"That sounds wonderful." Cathy felt better immediately. "Are you going to shower too, Michael?"

"Are you making me an offer I can't refuse?" He grinned.

Blushing furiously, Cathy gave him a quick jab in the ribs with her elbow.

"No?" He laughed. "Well, then I'm going to skip it. I'll go see what I can dig up for our rescue, okay? I'll meet you back here in fifteen minutes."

Never had Cathy tasted anything as good as the lukewarm lime punch. It went down smoother than champagne. She carried the glass out back and checked out the shower. It was just a shower head attached to the back wall of the store, screened by three walls about head high. She stood for a moment, frowning, weighing the pleasures of warm, fresh water against the perils of this primitive plumbing. The thought of soap and warm water won out.

She stepped inside, pulled her T-shirt over her head, stepped out of her shorts and panties, and unhooked her bra. She laid the whole pile carefully on a rock right next to the opening, flipped a towel over the top of the wall and turned on the water.

"Yikes!" Well, it wasn't warm, but it wasn't salty. She lathered herself from head to toe, then stood under the spray, sighing happily. Oh, this was heaven! Maybe she should have invited Michael. She giggled to herself at the thought of his bulk squeezed into this little cubby along with her, his shoulders, chest, thighs . . . Whoa! Her giggle dropped an octave, and she turned her face up to the spray. "That's gonna get you in trouble, Stephenson," she said into the stream of water, the words and spray calming the hot rush to a manageable level.

After another few delicious minutes she turned the water off, dried herself with the thin towel Gloria had given her, and reached outside. It was a shame to have to get back into these wet clothes, but her options were limited.

She quickly sorted through the small pile of clothes and then stopped short. Something was missing. She checked again. Shirt, panties, shorts, all present and accounted for. But where was her bra? "What the—"

Cathy hopped into what she had and stepped outside the makeshift shower. Across the alley was a group of boys about twelve years old, having a great game of shoot the can. Cathy watched the stone hit the can, and the can neatly topple into the dust. And then her eyes traveled back to the marksman and his slingshot. It was her bra!

Cathy ground her teeth and marched around the side of the building. She was working her way through a surprisingly colorful set of expletives when she ran smack dab into Michael. "Damn!"

He stared down at her, openmouthed. "I thought

for a minute there I'd run into a shipload of sailors," he said, eyeing her with newfound admiration. "That was quite a mouthful for a nice girl from Indiana."

"Stop putting down Indiana, Winters!" she shouted, poking him in the chest. "We know just as much as you New York types. We've just got more restraint, that's all!"

"I can tell," he answered softly, a grin tugging at the corner of his mouth.

Cathy took one look into his eyes and burst out laughing. She butted her head into his shoulder, leaning there and laughing while he held her and laughed with her, his breath lifting her damp hair.

"Well, gonna tell me what happened?"

"Later." She wrapped her arms around his waist and leaned back, smiling up at him. "What I want to know is, what's going to happen *next*? Did you find a phone? Did you get us rescued? What now?"

Michael took a deep breath, then shrugged. "I traded my Rolex for a sailboat. Guess it's still just you and me, kid."

Ten

"I don't think this was worth a Rolex!" Cathy threw the little wooden sailboat a suspicious glance. Then her eyes flew back to Michael's face like pigeons to their roost. He was security. Home. Everything she had.

"Hey, stop looking so worried. This is a trusty little catboat, and we're just heading across shallow water to the next cay."

If she was worried, Michael was anything but. Cathy could sense his excitement, made bolder and brasher by the challenge. He hopped onto the narrow deck and held to the mast as the boat swayed under his weight. "Looks watertight. Nice and steady. Come on board."

"Now?" she asked, wishing for a plane, a train, a helicopter, anything!

"Come on. We'll get a good start and make it to Little George Cay by nightfall. Here—" He held out one broad, suntanned hand.

Cathy could see the scratches, the cuts, the jagged rip of one nail, the dirt on his hands and arms. It all matched his torn shorts and stained canvas shoes. But he was grinning from ear to ear, laugh lines etched white against the tan of his skin. She could almost see the excitement pumping through his veins. If his three-piece-suit associates in New York could see him now, they would have him committed!

"You're sure there was no phone?" she asked one last time.

"Get on board, Indiana." He offered his hand again, reaching for her, impatient to be gone.

With a sigh Cathy took his hand and let him pull her onto the deck. The boat rocked, and she pushed Michael away for a good grip on the mast.

"You don't have to strangle the thing, Cathy. Just sit back, relax, and I'll talk you through the whole thing. Okay?"

"No," she muttered.

"Good. Now, you see that hollowed-out space back of the mast? Go sit down in there; that way you won't get hit by the boom."

"You hit me with a boom or anything else, Mr. Winters, and your days are numbered. I don't want to be here in the first place, and I certainly don't want to get bopped on the head, and—"

"Sit down, Cathy."

She tossed him an insolent salute and scooted toward the back of the boat. "Hey, wait a minute! There are feathers in here!"

"Sounds possible." Michael shrugged. "Fellow who sold me the boat said he used it to ferry chickens back and forth to market. That and an occasional pig or two. If you find a spare creature, hang on to it; we may need it for dinner tonight."

Cathy groaned. *This* from a man who probably had two dozen freshly starched and ironed white button-down shirts hanging in his closet at all times! She gingerly moved the toe of her sneaker around the bottom of the hollow.

Ignoring her, Michael leaned across to the dock, the muscles flexing in his arms, shoulders, and back, and untied the frayed rope. With a paddle he pushed them off, and maneuvered them toward open water. And then, grinning as if nothing gave him such pleasure, he sent the mainsail climbing to the head of the mast and let the wind take them. The little boat skidded across the tops of the waves, and the land fell away behind them.

"Bye," Cathy called forlornly to no one in particular. An egret lifted its head and then flapped on to a quieter cove. Cathy wished *she* had wings.

"Isn't this great?" Michael called over his shoulder, his grin flashing bright as the sun on the water. She had never seen anyone look so busy—and so happy—at the same time.

It made her feel downright ornery. "You're sure you know what you're doing?"

"Positive. I've been sailing since I was eight."

"Hmmph. And you're sure you know where we're going?"

"South by southwest. An easy sail, they said."

"Who's 'they'? The chicken man?" she scoffed.

"Want to steer?" He was feeling too damn happy to fight. Instead, he let go of the tiller and folded his arms loosely across his bare chest.

The little sailboat dipped sharply to port.

"No!" Cathy yelped. "You're doing fine. Great. Perfect!"

"Good. Then sit back and relax, keep low, and duck when I say duck." He winked. "And have a nice day." His laughter rolled out across the water, easy and clear as a river tumbling over rocks. Even his body looked different: muscles stretched and eager, skin bronzed and glistening with sweat, every move sure and quick and agile.

Cathy squinted at him. What was different? What had changed?

And then, as he leaned back, drenched with sunlight, grinning to himself as he trimmed the sail, she saw what it was: the tension was gone. The walls were down, the mask put away. He was having fun.

It was like seeing him for the first time, and for a moment it took her breath away. She wanted to say something, tell him how glad she was that he was happy, tell him how sexy he was when he laughed like that, tell him—heck, she wanted to *kiss* him! But she was too scared to move.

So she sat and watched him all afternoon, ducking when he told her to duck, trailing one hand in the water, and finally relaxing enough to hold the tiller for a few minutes at a time.

"How about something to eat?" Michael asked, digging into the basket the chicken man's wife had packed as part of the deal. "We've got conch fritters, 'corned' fish, plenty of fruit?"

"You take the tiller back and I'll take a banana, or some watermelon."

She waited for him to get a firm grip on the tiller

before she started to edge away, but he grabbed her around the waist with one hand, pulled her down on his lap, and kissed her hard on the mouth.

She broke away, flushed and laughing. "What was that for?"

" 'Cause I feel so damn good!"

"Well, you look damn good."

He tipped his head, his eyes shining with pleasure. "Well, thank you, ma'am!" And again his laughter boomed out over the quiet sea. "You look pretty good yourself." He winked. "Come 'ere."

"No way!" She laughed, settling herself back in her comfortable spot and fishing a banana out of the basket. "Save it, Mr. Winters. Get us to land and I'll consider your offer. Hmmm, would that be considered a hostile takeover?" she teased, one brow climbing mischieviously into her curly bangs.

"I'd rather think of it as a friendly merger, Ms. Stephenson."

In late afternoon the wind picked up and a dark line appeared on the horizon.

"Is that land?" Cathy asked hopefully, holding on with both hands.

"Afraid not, Indiana." Michael shaded his eyes with the flat of one hand. "Looks like a squall." He paused. "Heading our way . . ." he added, more to himself than to her. He looked around, judging distance, time, speed, and direction.

In seconds the rain clouds had raced toward them through an otherwise blue sky.

"Look, I'm going to turn east and try to outrun it, but I can't guarantee anything."

She gasped. "Thanks a lot. That makes me feel much better."

"Well, you wouldn't want me to lie, would you?"

"Of course I would! Lie or save me—that's your choice!" Her voice was rising like the wind, and panic beat in her chest. Wide-eyed, she watched the approaching curtain of rain. "Oh, Michael! What's going to happen?"

"We're going to get very wet, very soon, darlin'. I'm going to lower the sail. So just hold on, don't panic, it won't last long—"

His last words were blown away by the storm. In a matter of seconds she was soaked to the skin: shirt, shorts, hair, sneakers, all dripping water. The only blessing was that she couldn't see a thing, she could only hear the waves leaping and roaring around her. She held on. Eyes closed, mouth closed, chin tucked into her shoulders, she held on and prayed. Feathers floated around her ankles. The picnic basket tipped and bobbed. The boat jumped like a rodeo bronc.

And then the squall blew away. In the space of five minutes they had sailed into it and out of it, and once again the sky ahead was crystal blue, the water smoothing to ruffled silk. Cathy blinked twice, afraid to let go, afraid to move.

"Are you all right?" Michael asked.

Cathy heard the excitement in his voice. "No," she cried. "I'm not all right! I'm soaked, scared, bumped and bruised, hysterical—and if you don't stop grinning at me, I'm going to rip your head off!"

"Glad you're fine. Now, help me untangle the rigging and we'll get the sail back up." He was already hunkered down among the rope and cotton, the water dripping out of his thick dark hair and down his neck and back.

Cathy scowled, unnoticed, then swiped at a rivulet of rainwater running down her cheek. Oh, well, just another adventure in the continuing saga of Cathy and Michael. She pictured it just that way. Disaster headlines. With a loud, sincere groan she knelt down in three inches of water and helped unknot the rigging.

They shouldn't have bothered. Ten minutes after the squall passed, the wind died.

"Michael?" Cathy whispered, hushed by the stillness all around. "What happened now?"

"Trade wind's gone. It does that now and then at these latitudes."

"Then how do you sail a sailboat?" she asked, staring up at the limp white cotton.

Michael ducked his head and bit back his grin. "You don't, dear one."

"What *do* you do?" Fear made her persistent.

"You wait."

"Oh."

She lasted about ten seconds.

"Michael, we must be able to do *something*."

He shrugged. After a few minutes he reached for a hunk of watermelon and bit in, then spit the seeds out, one at a time, each one farther into the ocean, aiming carefully.

"That's a great talent, Michael, and one that's sure to stand us in good stead at some future date. But can't you think of anything that might help *now*?"

He laughed softly, reached a hand into the water, and flicked a few drops at her. "Relax, Indiana!"

"I don't want to relax!"

He handed her the paddle.

Glaring at him, Cathy yanked it out of his hands and started to paddle furiously. She paddled on one side, then the other, hard, digging the flat blade into the still, clear water. The sweat ran down her back and between her breasts. She panted with effort. Her ears rang. And nothing moved. They could have been glued onto this piece of blue sea, under this piece of blue sky.

"Are we *getting* anywhere?" Cathy asked.

"Hard to tell," Michael answered gently. "It's a big ocean and a little paddle."

"Oh, and you're just going to sit there with your hands folded behind your head, showing off your chest, while I try to save us?"

"The wind'll come back, Cathy. Until then you might as well take it easy—"

"I can't take it easy. I'm scared! It's already late afternoon"—she pointed at the sun on its downward arc—"and if I get stuck out here in the dark, I'm going to go crazy. Please, *do* something, Michael."

"Okay, okay," he whispered, calming her with a touch. "Here. Give me the paddle. Put on this hat and lean back, and I'll give it a try." He waited to see her follow orders, then knelt at the front of the boat and began paddling with a firm, steady stroke.

"Thank you," Cathy whispered to his broad back.

"My pleasure." He shook his dark head. Cathy was the most impatient, exasperating woman he'd ever met. And the most wonderful.

He paddled for a very long time.

Without landmarks or buoys or anything but water and sky all around, there was no way to know if they were even moving. Thinking of the strong, invisible currents in the water beneath them, Cathy was sure they were moving backward, farther and farther out to sea. Her heart hopped around like a rabbit in a cage.

"Michael," she called.

"What, hon?"

That sounded so safe and homey. "Nothing. I just wanted to check. . . . We're going to be all right, aren't we?"

He turned to face her, the sweat pouring into his eyes and down his bare chest, his grin steady as the beam in a lighthouse. "You bet. I wouldn't let anything happen to you, Indiana."

In the gathering dusk she smiled. "Thanks, pal."

"You're welcome." He smiled back at her.

She felt a tickle on the back of her neck, and brushed at it absently with one hand. And then the tickle turned into a breath, and her hair lifted off the nape of her neck, and there it was: the wind. Back again. The trade wind began to blow and the sail flapped, and Michael gave a shout of victory and the catboat came back to life.

"Michael, we're moving!"

"What do you call my hours of slaving with that damn paddle?" He laughed, leaning far back and using his whole weight to turn the boat into the wind. "Duck!" he shouted, and swung the boom over her head. The sail filled and little boat skimmed happily over the water, fanned into whitecaps again by the wind.

Cathy laughed and waved her hat and then ate a fritter to celebrate.

They sailed on into the dark.

Michael knew they'd missed Little George Cay, but he kept the boat headed southwest, hoping for another island, telling jokes, and singing to pass the time. He had a rich, pleasing baritone, and the first time he broke into song, Cathy stared at him in delighted surprise, then joined in on the chorus of 'Row, Row, Row Your Boat.' Unfortunately, other than that and a few obscene ditties, he seemed to know only Christmas carols. After the third go-round of "Jingle Bells," she couldn't sing she was laughing so hard.

Later she dozed off, arms crossed over the picnic basket, head pillowed on her arms. The wind was blowing steadily, the ship rocking gently as it sailed on, the breeze warm as a blanket. Michael watched her sleep, a smile curving his lips. He was exhausted, but somewhere in his chest, about heart high, there was a warm bloom of happiness.

He sailed all night. After a while his arms and back ached, his hands were bruised and sore from the paddling. Each touch of the tiller sent pain shooting up to his shoulders. His eyes felt like dry stones in his head. He wanted a cup of water so badly he could taste it . . . but not badly enough to disturb Cathy's sleep. *Cathy.* Just looking at her made him ache in ways that had nothing to do with paddling. Curly brown hair, round cheeks, the curve of her breasts to the arch of her foot, everything about her stirred him in strange unexpected ways. Name it, he thought to himself, but he shied away from the thought. Would not say it, even to himself. But the feeling grew and grew, as if to mock his reticence. Cathy, Cathy . . .

He must have fallen asleep, because the tiller

slapped at his hand, the boat dipped to starboard. "What?" His eyes snapped open. But tiredness sat on him like a dead weight. Looking up at the starry sky, he judged it to be about four in the morning.

"Michael?" Cathy called. "Everything okay?"

"Yes."

"I must have fallen asleep. I'm sorry. Are you okay?"

"I'm fine," he answered automatically, but then the exhaustion pressed in behind his eyes. "Listen, do you think you could take over for just a little while. An hour maybe?"

She wanted to say no in the worst way—the words almost jumped out of her mouth. But she had heard the strange, weary edge in his voice and could see the hunched outline of his shoulders in the dark. He must be dead tired, she knew, or he would not have asked.

So she said yes. "Just show me what to do."

He showed her how to hold the tiller, how to keep steady with the wind, nothing fancy, just enough to keep them heading in the right direction. "See that star?" he asked, pointing. "Just keep it straight ahead. And I'll be right here. Okay?"

"Sure." She nodded fast and wrapped her hand around the tiller.

Michael was asleep almost before he sat down.

In a minute Cathy's knuckles were white with strain, but she kept her eyes glued to the star ahead. She could not remember when she had felt this scared. No! To tell the truth, she could remember a number of times, all since that evening when she had first seen Michael!

Oh, Michael. She shook her head, confused. She didn't know whether to pray for rescue or cherish every shipwrecked second. That man, that gorgeous, irresistible, unpredictable man. That rat! Sleeping while she tried to steer this tiny, waterlogged little boat through the whole damn Atlantic Ocean, following a star! What was he doing sleeping at a time like this? What time was it anyway? Where *was* the star? Oh! She sighed with relief, there it was, straight ahead. . . .

Oh, Gap, was this all just going to turn into a story to tell around the dining room table on Thanksgiving and Christmas? When she grew old, would she forget? Would memories of Michael fade away like some old photograph, his face blurring in memory until she could no longer remember the exact color of his eyes, or the shape of his mouth, or his sudden heartstopping grin?

"Concentrate," she commanded. "Concentrate." But her thoughts wiggled around like so many worms: jumbled, disorganized, uncontrollable. Was she having the best time of her life? Or the worst? Did she want to find civilization in the next second? Or the next century? Was he wild? Or wonderful? Or both?

And did she love him?

The last thought stopped her short. Her heart skipped a beat. She had not meant to ask that, did not want to ask it. Or answer it. She slid him a sideways glance, one little glance in the dark, and yet the sight of him, asleep, long legs stretched out across the deck, an arm flung over his eyes, filled her with yearning. She wanted to do everything: touch him, kiss him, cover him with a blanket, tuck him in, throw herself on top of him—wake him and make him love her!

Nice thoughts for a girl from Indiana, she frowned. She needed a drink, just a sip of tepid coffee from the bottle in the basket. Could she get it? Stretching, her fingers just reached the lid. Holding tight to the tiller, she pulled it a little closer, edged the top up, felt around for the bottle. Where was it? Darn! Looking in, she saw it had tipped, and the coffee was now mingling with the seawater in the bottom of the boat. Damn!

And then she looked back ahead, and the star had disappeared.

Gone!

She looked around wildly, feeling lost, absolutely lost. Panicked. Frantic.

Huge sobs tore from her throat and there was nothing she could do to stop them.

"What?" Michael demanded, leaping awake, stumbling, finding a hold on the edge of the boat. "Oh, God, what? What is it, Cathy? Are you all right?"

"No," she sobbed. "I lost it. I lost the star. I don't know where we are. I—I lost it!"

"That's because the sun is coming up," he said softly, and wrapped his arms around her. "Look over your shoulder, love. See the light?"

Cathy felt her breath stop in her throat. "What?" she whispered, knowing he'd repeat the whole thing and go on to explain where they were and how and when. "What?" she whispered.

"Love," he whispered back only what mattered. "Love."

Eleven

"Michael, this is incredible!" Cathy sat with her chin resting on her knees, arms wrapped around her legs, bottom planted on the wet sand.

The sudden sight of a cay and their rough-and-tumble landing had left her no time to be embarrassed over his last words. "Love," he had called her. She stored it away and carefully kept her voice playful.

"Michael, are you listening? This is incredible. The more time we spend together, the fewer clothes I've got. I mean"—she threw her hands wide—"I started out a week ago in a sundress, shoes, sweater, underwear . . . carrying a purse, no less! And here I am in a pair of raggedy shorts and a T-shirt. And wet! I'm always wet! I spend more time in the water than Flipper!"

"But can you balance a ball on your nose?" He laughed, paying little attention to her complaining as he lugged the little catboat farther up onto the sand. Straining against the rope, muscles bunching with the effort, his body made her ache to touch him, ache and tremble with something she was afraid would be called lust.

When he stopped, she quipped, "Why don't you pull it up a little higher, Michael. Just another tug or two."

"You really like to see me sweat."

"Darn right."

"Well, I've had it." He flopped down onto the sand beside her, folding his arms behind his head. "I am beat, darlin'. That was one hell of a landing!"

"Those waves—" She shook her head at the memory. "Is everything ruined?"

"The food's all wet, but we've got plenty of fresh water and the matches are dry." He pulled the little waterproof tin out of one pocket and dropped it in her hand. "And the blanket will dry. All we've got to do is find something to eat."

"How about a phone? A motel with clean white sheets and an eighteen-inch color TV? A Burger King with large fries and a chocolate shake? An airport?"

"I'll keep my eye out." He smiled. Rolling onto one hip, he laid his head in her lap, the dampness of his thick dark hair chilling her thigh.

She drew her fingers through his hair, fingertips alert to the texture, the feel of his rough, shaggy mane. It was strangely erotic. And then she suddenly realized that he was growing a beard. She brushed the backs of her fingers against his cheek. Rough. Prickly. It made her oddly aware of his maleness, his potent sexuality, as if here on the beach some more primitive Michael was taking over, breaking through his polished, civilized shell.

"Sorry about that." He broke into her thoughts, rolling over so that his head was nestled between her thighs, his cheek pressed against her belly. "I know I must look like hell, but"—he shrugged—"no razor."

"I . . . I don't mind," she stuttered. "It's kind of nice. Different." She swallowed. "But nice."

"Thanks." He grinned. "I've got to admit it feels good, kind of wild and woolly, shipwrecked on some deserted island like Robinson Crusoe. Hell, I've always loved that book!"

Cathy was barely listening, her thoughts were racing so. For as long as he'd had no razor, *she'd* had no shampoo, no Dial, no nice little Lady Sunbeam of her own. What she must look like—

Just then he rolled toward her again, wrapping his arms around her waist and burying his face against her. "You smell so good, Cathy. So clean, like sea foam and sunshine."

Her whole body shivering with awkwardness, Cathy could barely speak. "Thanks," she finally managed to say. She tried to ease out from under him, but he held her tight.

"Don't go yet. You know, Cathy, I've never felt so good. I mean I feel *good*, alive, healthy, fantastic!" He leaned back and gave a little chuckle deep in his throat. "You know how much time I usually spend working out in a gym on the fiftieth floor of a modern Manhattan high rise, full of the best equipment? Every Tuesday and Thursday I have a massage to try to unknot the knots, ease the strain." His blue eyes were focused somewhere to the right of her cheek, his brow drawn low. "You know what? None of it works."

Then he gave that low chuckle again. "I wouldn't tell my masseur, or the guy who runs the gym, but it never came close to this. Hell—" He laughed, looking right in her eyes. "Just think how many major industries we could ruin if we could package this! Good-bye health spas, cosmetics, deodorant soaps. The whole advertising industry would hate us."

The thought gave him great pleasure, and he lay there, grinning from ear to ear.

His mood was contagious, and she smiled back at him as she traced the curve of his mouth. "I must admit, Winters, you do look good."

"Not as good as you, darlin'," he answered, his voice grown suddenly husky. "Your skin is smooth and soft as a peach, sweeter, smoother, with a little color here"—he touched her nose, her cheeks—"and here, and here." The corner of his mouth tugged down in a wily grin. "And here." He pressed a blunt finger to her throat, trailed it down to the rise of her breast. "And here." Lifting onto one elbow, he pressed his lips where his touch had been, his mouth warm and wet and startlingly erotic.

Cathy felt his mouth trailing wet kisses down her throat, and found herself teetering on the edge of her invisible line. Ecstasy beckoned from the other side.

She should stop him. There was no future in this. She knew better. She was a realist. She was a responsible, sensible—

"Oh, Cathy," Michael groaned, his breath flowing

down over her breasts so that her nipples tingled and tightened. Stars sparked behind her eyes. She arched her back, took a trembly little breath . . . and leapt right over her line.

His body read her response immediately. It sent Michael staggering back with her away from the water, up to the dry, warm, smooth sand, and he dropped to his knees, still holding her, laid her down, and covered her slim body with his own.

She took his weight with joy, loving the solid strength of him, the heaviness that meant his bones, muscles, flesh, and form. She could hardly breathe, but every shallow breath filled her head with his smell, salt dried in his hair, suntan oil, and sweat.

Loving it, wanting more, she slipped her tongue out to stroke along his rough cheek. He turned his face, nipped the tip of her tongue between his teeth, then teased her with hot, hungry kisses. Starting at her mouth and working his way down, he tasted her warm, silken flesh, licking, kissing, pressing his mouth to the curve of her collarbone, the fullness of her breasts, the tight buds of her nipples through her tank top.

Then, with cool, slow hands, he lifted the bottom edge of her shirt and pulled it up, exposing her pale breasts, their puckered rose-colored tips. His mouth closed over one nipple, wet and hot and rasping in slow, maddening circles that made her writhe with pleasure. She lifted her legs and locked them around his hips, pulling him closer, but he arched back against her legs, letting only his mouth touch her, until he rubbed his head between her breasts, whispering, "Slow, slow, Cathy."

"No, come to me, Michael," she cried softly, her voice hoarse and unfamiliar, her hands sliding hungrily over his back and shoulders. "Come, come here," she demanded softly, trembling, aching, but he knelt over her, touching her lightly from throat to belly, his hands circling in delight over her hot skin, until they slid down and tugged at the waistband of her shorts.

She lifted her hips between his thighs, relishing how well they fit together, keeping her hips up even as she moved and circled.

He gave a deep husky laugh and pressed her down, the sand warm beneath her bare buttocks, and him so warm and heavy on top.

"You too," she whispered, and he slipped out of his shorts and for the first time, after all this time together, she saw him naked. He was so perfect, so breathtaking. She just had to touch him. *Had to!* He was so beautiful, his body so wonderfully carved into muscle and sinew and flesh. She could not stop looking. Couldn't! And then . . . slowly he lowered himself on top of her, and she could feel him from chest to toes, pressed against her, and she let her head fall back, her eyes closed, weak with desire. Helpless.

Yearning. Waiting.

His breath whispered in her ear, "You are so beautiful, so beautiful, Cathy."

She sobbed with impatience, "Now, now, Michael, please now!" as he whispered, "Slow, Cathy, slow," and touched her everywhere with teasing touches. Finally, crying, trembling, and shaking, she pulled him deeper into her until he filled her with wild unbelievable feelings, tremors and tears, and a delicious joy that exploded out of her in cries of sheer ecstasy and madly abandoned laughter.

Michael lay panting on top of her, holding her tight, his weight heavy now that he lay sprawled and spent. The breath was squeezed from her chest, and she held him, breathless, loving being scrunched, until he lifted himself up on both hands and smiled down at her. "I didn't squash you, did I?"

She couldn't speak, could only smile up into his eyes, where she saw herself, irrevocably changed by their loving.

Oh, here they were, not rolling and tumbling and caught in some wild frenzy soon over with, but grinning at each other in pure happiness. Connected. Looking into each other's eyes and seeing something miraculous reflected there.

Placing a hand on either side of his face, Cathy drew his head down toward her and kissed him gently on the mouth, her tongue tracing the curve of his lips.

"So," she said finally, "that's what all the fuss is about, hmmmm?"

"Oh, love—" he breathed, lifting his face just enough to dust kisses on her cheeks and chin. "Oh, my love—"

"Shhh," she said, putting a finger on his lips. "You don't have to put words to it, Michael. I'm happy to take it for what it is . . . a fairy tale . . . a magic moment."

He kissed her on the lips, stopping her words, her breath, then brushed his words against her cheek. "Don't you know, Cathy? Don't you know it's the truth? I love you." He kissed her ear. "I love you. I thought you knew."

And curving up to him, pressing her mouth to his bronze warm skin, she answered. "Yes, yes, and I love you too."

Twelve

They lay there for a long time, sprawled on the empty beach, content to listen to the surf and each other's breathing. When Cathy shifted on the sand, Michael pulled her back close, pillowing her curly head on his shoulder. "Don't go yet, don't move. I'm too happy."

Cathy rolled onto her side and kissed his chest. "Me too. Don't worry. I'm not going anywhere."

But she was the first to break the spell. She worried that someone was going to come strolling down the beach and find them lying there, bare and blushing. Someone on their way to market, or out fishing, or kids come to swim.

The thought got her up and moving. She dashed down to the water and jumped in, splashing and swimming, dipping under to wash her hair and springing up again, water cascading down her golden body.

Michael watched her from his bed in the sand, his eyes dark with pleasure and desire.

When she walked back up and picked up her shorts, he leaned up on one elbow. "Don't. Come on back here. Let's make love again and then I'll find you a sarong and wrap you up, island girl."

"Come find the sarong first." She laughed, stepping into her shorts and pulling on her top. She turned and faced him, hands planted on her hips. "Well, Mr. Crusoe, I'm hungry and wet for a change. What are you going to do about it?"

"Sleep," he replied, dropping one arm over his eyes.

Cathy tiptoed to the water's edge, caught a little sandcrab. Tiptoed back. Knelt. Placed the crab on Michael's chest.

It was hard to tell whether Michael or the crab moved faster. "What the hell!" he yelled, jumping to his feet. The three of them raced for the surf, the crab disappearing and Michael ducking Cathy until she leapt up against his chest, wrapped her legs around his hips, and buried her face against his neck. "Stop! I give, I give," she sputtered.

"Oh . . . there *is* a Santa Claus," Michael said, carrying her just to where the sand was dry before he made love to her again.

By mid-afternoon, no one had passed by, but Cathy's tummy was grumbling with hunger. "Michael. Michael . . ." She poked him. "We have got to find something to eat. Now!"

"A loaf of bread, a jug of wine, and thou . . ." he quipped, lazy and grinning like a fox.

"Enough 'thou' for now. I want the bread and wine, Winters!"

"Heartless woman." But he got up, pulled on his shorts, and tossed her her clothes. "Come on. We'll explore."

They walked along the beach again, finding tide pools and rocks and long stretches of pink sand, but no sign of people. Inland was a dense green garden. They wandered in, avoiding the sharp edges of the palmettos, and walked through the cool interior, stilling the loud cacaphony of bird calls with their presence. "Sorry, guys, just passing through," Michael said, laughing.

Back on the beach they continued their circle, the sun sauntering on its arc through the blue and dazzling sky.

All of a sudden Cathy yelled, "Look, look there; there's something on the beach!"

They sprinted off together, but then Michael stopped, laughing, his hands resting on his knees. "Relax, darlin', there's no hurry."

"Why?"

"Because it's us, dear one. Our boat. Our basket."

"You mean we've come all the way around? There's no one but us? No little village? Nothing?"

"Nice, huh?"

"Except for the fact that I'm starving."

"No problem." He gave a mock bow and strode off down the beach, calling over his shoulder in a thick French accent, "What would Madame care for? Conch? Mussels? Crab? Yellowtail? Fresh coconut milk to drink? Papaya for dessert?"

Cathy caught up with him and grabbed him around the waist. "Can you really do this, Michael?"

"Yes," he said down to her upturned face. "I can

do anything. Haven't you learned that yet? And so can you. Come on."

"Me?"

"You bet. What's Robinson Crusoe without his pal Friday?"

So he taught her how to find conch and crawfish, and how good crabs could taste and, in the days that followed, how to fish with a long, pointed stick, and even how to dive for lobsters.

That first night they collected wood for a fire, carefully used one of the matches, and dried the blanket and then sat together, her head on his shoulder, his arm around her waist, watching the flames and the sea beyond.

"Is this really happening?" she whispered, nestling against him. "If it's a dream, don't wake me up. Let me sleep a hundred years, and wake only to your kiss."

"Wrong fairy tale," he said. But he kissed her anyway.

Their passion woke instantly. It was never far away. Beneath the most ordinary action lay an awareness of each other's body, each other's response. He could bend to pick up a stick, and she would have to reach out and touch his bare thigh. She would shake out the blanket, and he would come close behind and kiss the nape of her neck. Her shivers made him tremble. His heat made her burn.

She could barely look at him without wanting him. The sight of his bare chest drove her mad, and she would touch, kiss, touch until they were down on the sand. She would get up, swim, try a little fishing, and she would see the water running in rivulets down through his dark hair, down his chest and belly, and she would have to go swipe at them with the tip of her tongue, and there they would be, down on the hot, smooth surface of the rocks. She got a penny-size bruise on one buttock that way, and when he saw it he had to kiss it and make it better.

It was a fever. It rose and fell like delirium, interrupting the most casual talk, the most innocent act. Everything was erotic. The way he walked. The way she smiled. The swell of his muscles. The curve of her breasts.

After the first few days she gave up wearing her top and grew almost as dark as he was. Even her breasts tanned, the nipples changing from rose to plum. And he nibbled at them like some sweet fruit, driving her mad.

"The morning's the best," she murmured, waking in the circle of his arms, the stars just fading above them, the sea glowing like some huge pale lantern at the edge of the world.

Then it was noon, the hot sun baking the sand, their skin salty, their hair salty, their bodies glowing with lovemaking, and the cool sea waiting. "No . . ." She laughed, "Noon is best."

At dusk they sat with hips, sides, shoulders touching and watched the sun go down behind their island, and the sea gather the darkness like skirts into her lap. Cathy's heart would ache with joy, the joy of such beauty and this man she loved to share it. "Evening's best!"

And then there were the nights!

Each day was perfect, and she never thought beyond that perfect day.

Then one evening they saw a yacht out on the horizon. It was a tiny white shape, close enough for rescue.

"A fire!" Cathy yelled, and Michael was already up, tossing sticks and brush into a pile, fumbling in his pocket for the matches.

"Here!" He tossed her the tin as he dashed for wood.

"Okay!" Her heart was pounding. She pulled open the tin, took out one match, struck it. Then she stopped. Her hands started to shake. She stood there frozen, watching the white yacht edge along the distant horizon. Farther and farther away. Almost gone. "Oh, Michael," she whispered, "Michael, what should I do?" But he wasn't there to answer.

She blinked, counted out ten matches, tucked them in the waistband of her shorts, and tossed the rest into the surf.

"Oh, no!" she gasped, watching them get swept away.

"What's the matter?" He ran up, spun her around so he could see her face. "Are you all right?"

She shook her head, her face sad. "I dropped them . . . in the water . . . the matches," she cried.

He looked over her head. The yacht had vanished. "It doesn't matter," he whispered. "It's all right. Don't cry, Cathy, it's all right."

She could not explain what she had done, or why. She felt like a cheat, a liar. He believed her ploy, and she didn't have the nerve to tell him the truth. All evening she sat there, stiff and miserable, until he, trying to comfort her, pulled her close, hugging and nuzzling.

"It's all right, Cathy," he promised. "There'll be another ship. Or we can start out tomorrow and look for a cay with people, a phone. I'm sorry, dear one, so sorry. I didn't know how much you wanted to be rescued. I was thinking only of myself." He paused, his voice gone suddenly husky. "I was thinking only of how happy I am."

She jumped into his lap, knocking him flat on his back in the sand, laughing and crying so that she knew he must think she was crazy. But she didn't care. "Michael, oh, Michael, I love you! I love you so much." She kissed his mouth and his beard, the hollow of his throat, his chest.

"Good, great!" He laughed, startled into an arousal so strong it made his toes curl. "And whatever caused this sudden lust, I bless it. Yes—" He pulled her down tight against his warm, hard body and pulled off her shorts.

Ten little matches scattered on the sand.

"What the hell?"

"I couldn't help it," she whispered against his shoulder. "I needed one more night with you here . . . alone. I couldn't bear for it to end."

He gave a whoop of happiness and hugged her tight. "I'm glad, so glad, Cathy!" He tugged his fingers through her hair, slid them lovingly down the slope of her back. "And I have a confession to make too."

Instantly curious, she tipped her head to one side. "What?"

"Remember the day the kids turned your bra into a slingshot? Well . . . there was a phone on that island."

Frowning, she counted the days back in her head. "But that was over a week ago! Way back at the start—"

"Yes."

"And you didn't use it? Not even to call the office? Not even for business?"

The grin that was tugging at the corner of his mouth climbed to his blue eyes. "Not even for business, Cathy."

"Then I think you acted quite nobly, and in our mutual best interest." She smiled, opening her arms. "Come get your reward, Winters."

When she came back from shell collecting down near her favorite little cove the following afternoon, she found him sitting on the sand, hands wrapped around his knees, looking out to sea. It was unusual to find him so still, so still and serious-looking, and she stopped in her tracks. But she knew what he was thinking. She had been doing the same thinking down at the cove.

Seeing the yacht yesterday had brought the world back, if only to the edge of their horizon. Now they could no longer be content with their perfect days, but had to think of uncertain tomorrows. Should they light a signal fire? Should they sail to the next cay? Were people worried about them, looking for them? Did they have more to think about than just their own pleasure?

She stomped along the sand, troubled by her thoughts.

"Hi." Michael gave her a lopsided grin.

She came to a stop behind him. Dropping her treasures in his lap, she knelt and kissed the top of his head, burying her face in his thick dark hair. How much longer could this last?

"Hi, yourself." She wrapped her arms around him, locking her hands together over his chest. She could feel his heart beating.

"Don't think about everything, Michael. Not now. Just make love to me."

"My pleasure." He laughed, pulling her down over his shoulder and cuddling her in his lap. His hands traced the now-familiar curves and valleys of her body, teasing, adoring, drawing pleasure in their wake.

Her mouth drank his kisses and gave hungry ones back.

Their bodies melted together, becoming one until she couldn't tell where her flesh ended and his began.

"How can this just keep getting better and better?" she gasped, nipping at his lower lip with sharp little teeth.

"Practice makes perfect!" he murmured, his words strangled by passion.

When the gust settled into a light breeze, and they were both half sane again, they swam over to the cove and went fishing.

"These days were wonderful," Cathy said, standing quietly thigh-deep in the crystal-clear water. She looked up at him and gave him a dazzling smile. "Thank you for these days, Michael. For the freedom, the adventure, for teaching me how to fish."

"You're welcome," he replied just as seriously. "You're a good student."

"Thank you."

"And a good friend." He said it softly and it carried a secret meaning, a meaning she completely and totally understood.

"You too," she whispered.

His eyes locked on her face. And then he grinned. "And a good lover."

"A *great* lover." She grinned back.

"A great lover," he agreed, splashing her.

"Yes, and a good fisherman!" She laughed, splashing him back.

"Good fishermen don't splash." He leapt across the waves at her like a kid, drenching her with a huge splash as he landed in a belly flop. The fish streaked away like underwater bullets.

"Oops." He shrugged. "Fruit for lunch."

"You know, Michael, Gap wouldn't believe this if she saw me," Cathy mused. She had just shimmied down a palm trunk with two fresh coconuts.

"But she'd approve?"

"Oh, yes! She'd love it. And she would love you too."

"Will she?" he asked, carefully changing tense.

"Yes, she will." Cathy nodded. "She will."

That night they lit the fire with the second out of the nine matches left. There was a good strong breeze off the ocean, and the sand flies had disappeared. The sky was polka-dotted with stars, and everything was perfect.

"Reminds me of nights out on the cape," Michael said, looking out to sea.

"I've never been there," Cathy answered softly. "Is it beautiful?"

"Yes. It used to be even more so, before all the tourists. But my folks have fifty-five acres overlooking the sound, and that's still lovely." He turned his dark head, his eyes seeking hers. "You'll like it."

She nodded, feeling like a little hand had tightened around her heart. "Will I?" She smiled brightly.

"Yes," he assured her.

"Great!"

"Do you like modern art?" he asked as they strolled hand in hand along the pink sand at dawn.

The question did not surprise her. She understood. "Some. I like Rothko. And Frank Stella. But I love the Impressionists. I'm mad about Degas, Monet, Cézanne, Van Gogh . . . and Mary Cassatt. I love her women in their white dresses, all that light—"

"Andy Warhol?"

"Okay."

"Motherwell?" he paused. "I have a Motherwell hanging over the stairwell in my New York apartment."

"Well, I'm not sure about Motherwell." She paused. "I could let you know."

"Good."

"Do you eat pasta?" Cathy asked as they nibbled away at some roasted crawfish.

"I like pasta." He shrugged. "Cannelloni. Ravioli if it's homemade, especially with feta cheese."

"Oh." She made a face he did not see. "Sounds interesting."

"It's good. But I love Oriental food."

"Yes," she agreed happily, "me too. Chinese. Spareribs and egg rolls, wonton soup—"

"That's okay." He waved it away. "But have you ever eaten Szechuan? Thai? Vietnamese?"

"Vietnamese?" she repeated in disbelief.

"Great stuff! Especially the soups. They even prepare what they call dry soups. Delicious."

"Sounds . . . wonderful," she answered skeptically. "How do you feel about cheeseburgers?"

"Never touch beef."

"Oh, of course," she said. "Silly me."

The next morning she was shoulder-deep in the waves, washing her hair and singing, "I'm gonna wash that man right out of my hair," at the top of her voice as Michael swam laps nearby.

"You are beautiful," he said, floating by.

"Thank you, sir," she sang, feeling beautiful and very turned on. The sight of his hard, bronze body flashing through the waves always did that to her. Every time. There was something about the broad shoulders, the dark thick hair, the wide, curved bands of muscle across his chest and shoulders. With each stroke the muscles bunched and hardened, then stretched and smoothed. It was hypnotizing, the rhythm of his body. On this next lap she would just reach out and touch his chest, his flank, his thigh. . . .

She did, and he veered toward her, dove, and

caught her around the legs, lifting her clear out of the water as he surfaced.

"Stop! Put me down! Michael—"

He slid her slowly down the front of his body, slowly, holding her tight against him. By the time her toes touched sand, she was panting with arousal. "Michael, Michael," she whispered, her mouth searching hungrily for his lips, his tongue.

"Oh, I am glad you love this as much as I do!" He gave a deep, husky laugh and carried her, legs wrapped around his hips, out of the water and up onto dry sand.

"By the way," he asked later, drawing a hand lazily up the inside of her thigh, "do you like dogs?"

"Cats," she answered, purring with happiness.

That evening they used the sixth match out of the ten.

Michael lit the fire, put the lobsters on to cook, and then sat on the sand, hugging his knees.

Cathy came over and sat beside him, one arm draped over his bare broad shoulders, her cheek pressed against his warm skin.

"You know," he said reluctantly, finally putting into words everything she had been thinking for the past few days. "We're going to have to leave." He drew a deep breath and let it out slowly, keeping his head down. "We haven't got much water left. And only four matches—"

"I know." She nodded sadly. "I am so sorry. I should have kept twelve . . . fifteen. . . ."

"It's not your fault. A few more days, but we would have had to get going sooner or later. Besides, people must be worried . . . searching. The world beckons. . . ."

"I don't want the world. I want only you."

He grinned and kissed her nose. "And I want only you. That doesn't have to change."

"Maybe . . ." she answered softly. But she heard the "have to."

"Hey, pal, trust me! Okay?"

She smiled at him, but inside she was uneasy. Trust him? She would trust him with her soul if he'd let her. But he never said anything definite about their future. "Sure. How could I say no to the man who taught me to fish?"

"Right." He nodded. He was smiling, his handsome face lit by that familiar smile—the smile that warmed her, that had become her sun and moon. But she couldn't help remembering it was the same smile that sold magazines to millions of single women.

They set sail the next morning.

Cathy had her shells tucked in the bottom of the basket, and she carried the palm-frond fan she had woven to battle the mosquitoes. She wore her shorts and top and in her hair a piece of tortoiseshell Michael had found and carved for her.

Michael looked dark and solid and slightly wild and untamed with his torn shorts and shirt, beard, and bare feet.

They headed southwest again, catching the trade

wind in their sail and tacking swiftly through a light chop.

Just before dark they saw an island, a large one, and as they sailed around the southern tip, there were boats, fishermen, and a dock.

"Hello!" Michael called, waving an arm above his head.

"Watch de way, Papa! Watch de way!" an old man, dark-skinned with gray hair, yelled back, swinging an arm out to the left.

At that instant a huge outcropping of coral appeared just beneath the crystal surface of the water on the starboard side.

Michael yelled, "Duck!" swung the boom, and brought the catboat sharply to port.

Amid cheers from the fishermen, they sailed on in toward shore.

"Thanks for the warning," Michael said as Cathy white-knuckled the edge of the boat.

"No problem! Dat's one tricky way. Peoples sink out dere all de time. Does make fishing private, though."

"Well, we don't want to disturb your fishing, but we sure could use some food, fresh water, a phone."

"No phone hereabouts, Papa, but food and water we've got. Tie up de boat and make your way down de dock."

Cathy hopped onto the dock as Michael tied up. "Michael," she whispered when he stepped up next to her, "what are we going to use for money?"

"Haven't figured that out yet. But don't worry. Papa'll take care of everything."

"Oh, I love that: 'papa.' " She giggled, wrapping

her arm around his waist so that their hips bumped playfully as they walked. "Papa!"

The store was a tiny shack filled to the roof with an amazing collection of canned goods, lanterns, lures, shells, and baskets. There did not seem to be anyone there.

"Hello?" Cathy ventured. "Anyone home?"

A young woman appeared in a back window, waved, and came around front. "Sorry. I didn't hear you come up. Dis place don't get too many visitors." She smiled shyly, a beautiful welcoming smile.

Cathy smiled back.

Michael got right down to business. "We've got a problem," he said, spreading both hands wide. "We capsized and have no money, but we could sure use some food, water, and directions to an island with a phone."

"You take what you need," the girl offered simply. "And I be happy to give directions. Here, I draw you a map—"

"Listen, I have a knife. I could trade you the knife for the food."

"A man shouldn't rightly be out on the sea without a good knife. No, you just bring it by some later time. I'm not goin' anywheres."

"Thank you," Michael said. "We will do that."

"No problem."

"Thanks." Cathy gave her all she had, a smile, in return.

They slept the night on the beach, but chastely, at far ends of the blanket, aware that there were other people on this island. They had left their own little paradise behind and were heading back to civilization. Even though across the blanket they held hands, Cathy felt the interlude coming to an end.

"It's pretty here, isn't it?" Michael said.

Cathy heard the wistfulness in his voice. "Beautiful. We've seen a lot of beautiful places."

"Yes," he nodded, looking up at the stars. "And there are others. Paris. Lucerne. Melbourne. Hong Kong, in their own way. You'd like them, Cathy."

"I'm sure I would. The world's full of beautiful places. I know one about an hour's ride outside of Bloomington."

"I bet that's beautiful too. And Cape Cod. The Maine coast. Nantucket. Even Manhattan, from fifty stories up."

"How about Manhattan from right down at street level?"

"Well . . ." He turned his head and winked. "It does have its moments, but I'm not sure beautiful is the adjective I'd choose. Exciting, maybe. Vital. Challenging."

"That sounds like how you'd describe Michael Winters," she teased.

He looked at her. His dark brows drew together over cobalt eyes. "Which Michael Winters?" he said softly.

Cathy caught her lip between her teeth, thinking that one over. "Is there more than one?" she asked, watching for his response.

He rolled onto one hip, pillowing his dark head on the crook of one arm, looking at her. He had all his defenses down. No mask. No wall. Just him. "I think so, Cathy. Maybe. I know I'm different now from who I was a short while ago. I've been happy here with you."

"Aren't you happy there?"

"In a different way. I don't know if you'd understand."

"Try me."

He gave a low laugh deep in his throat. "I don't know if I can explain it. That's the truth."

"Well, can't both be real, Michael?"

He looked at her, not smiling, his eyes as dark as the velvet sky above them. "I don't know, Cathy."

She swallowed, shrugged, then took his hand again and squeezed it tight. "Well, we'll just wait and see, Papa. I'm not goin' anywheres."

In the morning, at "day clear" as the islanders called it, they set sail for a cay with a phone. Cathy was the navigator, and she sat holding the map the girl had drawn. For a moment she had an overwhelming desire to do with it just what she had done with the matches: dump it into the water, watch it float away, leave them stranded alone together—

But this time she knew life could not be that simple.

Thirteen

The island was quiet and secluded, but the dock that awaited Cathy and Michael was well maintained and dotted with several small dinghies and sailboats.

"Well, here we are," Michael said, lowering the sail.

"Yes," Cathy answered, her eyes darting from Michael's face to the thick cluster of palms beyond the beach. Looking at him for longer than a few seconds at a time was not a good idea, she had decided. Not right now. Trees were far safer.

"Civilization is a phone call away."

"That close?" Her eyes swung back to Michael's face and she fought the wave of sadness that overcame her. This was crazy. She should be rejoicing. They were headed for home, for safety and security. But she didn't feel safe or secure. She felt frightened and downright miserable.

A muscle jumped along Michael's jaw. He looked

away, studying the scene before them. "Pretty island," he said nonchalantly, looping the rope through
a ring attached to the dock.

"Maybe you should buy it," Cathy teased, but her
attempt at a joke fell flat.

"Hey, Indiana," Michael said, his fingers locking
around hers as he helped her out of the boat. "Don't
worry. This is just another beginning, another adventure together. Who knows what's ahead?"

"You're right, sorry." She nodded, forcing a little
smile. "So, where to?"

"Up this way." He took her hand and they headed
toward a carefully tended path that led off through
the palms. They walked silently, the only sounds
those of the creatures who lived in the dense foliage
that spread off on either side.

"Up there," Michael said a few minutes later, and
Cathy looked ahead to a clearing where sunshine
poured down on green lawns.

"Who lives here?"

Michael shrugged. "Someone who bought the island for a private vacation spot. Someone with a
telephone."

As they neared the clearing the house became
visible, a large, open structure with broad verandas
welcoming the sunshine. It was beautiful—spacious
and well kept—a tasteful, expensive reflection of the
island's beauty.

They walked silently across the lawns and up three
wide steps to the front door. Cathy clung tightly to
Michael's hand.

He looked down at her and grinned. "You've sur-
vived bombings and sunken ships and black nights

on deserted islands—and a beautiful, civilized estate scares the hell out of you. Is that how they raise women in Indiana?"

Cathy wanted to turn it all into a joke, but she just couldn't manage it. "I have a feeling there's more danger here," she said softly.

Michael dropped her hand and wrapped his arm around her shoulders, hugging her body into his side. "It's okay, Cathy," he whispered into her hair. "Honest, it'll be okay."

The door opened at the first knock and Cathy and Michael were greeted by a smiling young woman dressed in a crisp uniform. "Yes?" she said.

"We were shipwrecked," Michael began as Cathy peered into the cool, bright interior. "Our yacht blew up, and we need to use a phone—"

"Michael!" came a cry from the next room. "Michael Winters! Oh, my God—" And to Cathy's amazement, a tall, slender woman swept around the corner and threw herself into his arms.

Michael gave a low, rumbling laugh of surprise and pleasure as the woman rested her slender, manicured fingers on his shoulders and kissed him on both cheeks. "Michael, you are alive! The whole world's been looking for you."

"Marissa!" Michael said. "What incredible luck!"

"Luck has nothing to do with it, Michael darling," the woman replied. "It's the fates bringing us together again." She laughed her musical laugh, sounding rich and exotic.

To Cathy, it was all a part of a dream, or some movie in which she'd suddenly been cast as an extra. Her heart skipped a beat and she squeezed Michael's hand.

"Cathy," he said, "I want you to meet a friend of mine, Princess Marissa Aufhammer."

"Princess," Cathy repeated in amazement. But why should she still be surprised by anything that happened?

Marissa shook her head as she laughed, and long black hair swung across her narrow shoulders. "Cathy, I'm Marissa to you, just plain Marissa. Michael and I met eons ago at the home of a mutual acquaintance, and we've been fast friends ever since. And now I get to play a part in his rescue. This is so exciting! Better than the cinema!" She hugged Cathy warmly. "Now, come, come, come, you two, and tell me exactly how you ended up here on my doorstep."

She waved them both into a sunny room off the entry. It was filled with wicker furniture, beautiful art, and looked out onto gardens and a swimming pool bordered in the distance by the untouched island greenery. "Iced teas, yes?" she ordered, "and something sweet. Wonderful. Now, tell me all."

When Michael had finished the story, Marissa crossed one long leg over the other and shook her head. "My, my, that's quite a tale. Of course, I heard about the yacht being blown sky high; you must have been terrified. And furious."

"I imagine the sheikh had similar feelings," Michael said. "But"—he shrugged and winked at Cathy —"we made the best of it."

"How lovely it is that I've managed to be squeezed in on the end of your adventure. When the magazines write about this, will I get credit for being your rescuer?"

"It would certainly make good copy," Cathy said.

"The Great American Bachelor Rescued by a Princess." The light words stuck in Cathy's throat and she covered it up with a swallow of tea.

Michael looked over at her but remained silent.

"Well," the princess said quickly, filling the sudden awkward silence, "first things first. I'm sure you would both love a hot shower and some lunch. Jessa"—she rang a bell—"please show Mr. Winters to the guest wing. You may use my suite, Cathy. If you don't find everything you need, just ring for Jessa."

Cathy was ushered off into the sumptuous splendor of the princess's bedroom before she could say No! Stop! Wait! And what was she thinking? What could she possibly want to complain about? Her own ingratitude embarrassed her. But somewhere deep inside she felt her heart tightening, squeezing itself into a miserable little knot. No, she wanted to say. Stop! Wait! I'm happy with everything the way it is.

But instead, she obediently stepped under the hot spray of the princess's elegant shower, and sadly washed away the sand and smells of paradise.

"Cathy—" Michael stood up abruptly, his smile lighting his face. "You look beautiful."

She stood in the doorway dressed in a gauzy white caftan that Jessa had laid out on the bed. It was cool and lovely and floated down over her tan breasts and hips. She felt as if she were smothering.

"Thanks." She gave him a wry smile. "But clothes are going to take some getting used to."

"I know what you mean." Michael laughed, enduring the unaccustomed rub of slacks and a knit shirt.

Looking at him, Cathy let her imagination strip it all away, leaving the beauty of his body as she knew it. Her eyes lit and sparkled with mischief. "I have an idea: let's leave them all here in a pile and go for a swim; I hear the ocean calling."

He grinned. "What, and undo all the pleasure of that hot shower?"

"I can think of greater pleasures," she answered, slipping one hand inside the collar of his shirt and stroking his warm smooth skin.

Michael groaned and grinned and pulled her tight against him. "Behave, woman! Our hostess will be back in a second."

"Then we'd better act fast!" But they were not fast enough. Marissa caught them in their embrace, and chased them apart with that little tinkling laugh of hers.

"Well, there you are, looking much more civilized! Now, why don't we relax out on the terrace with a light lunch?"

Michael put a hand under Cathy's elbow, and that simple formal gesture made her cringe. It was like the clothing: too many layers of civilized behavior suddenly coming between them. She wanted to turn time back, stop the hands of the clock ticking in the hallway and spin them back, taking her and Michael back to their island and their sand and their blanket under the sun.

Jessa brought them each a glass of wine and they sat silently at the glass-topped table, their eyes seeking each other and trying to avoid contact at the same time.

Cathy took a large gulp of wine and set her glass

back on the table. The ring of crystal filled the silent, sun-splashed room.

Marissa looked from one to the other. "You must be exhausted, the two of you. Look at you, you're nearly too tired to talk. Food will help," she insisted, and smiled as Jessa returned carrying a huge white bowl of conch stew.

"Marissa, you're wonderful to take care of things for us," Michael said.

"Oh, dear me, no one will ever take care of things for you, Michael, of that I'm quite sure. But it is nice to be able to have a small part to play in this drama. And I have another surprise. I called over to Marsh Harbor and they are sending your helicopter over. Soon you'll be home!"

Helicopter! Cathy looked up, startled out of her silence. "Helicopter?"

Michael stiffened, his skin gone white under his tan, his hand clenched around the stem of his wineglass. "You already made the call?" he asked softly.

"Why, yes . . . I haven't done anything wrong, have I?" she asked with concern. "Here I thought I was being so clever and helpful, arranging the final stage of your rescue—"

"That was kind of you, Marissa."

"But you're not happy, not either one of you," she said, looking from Cathy to Michael and back again. "Oh, I have done something wrong. It was a mistake, an indiscretion, no?"

"It was perfectly fine, Mari," Michael assured her, reaching across the table to pat her hand. "As always, you were being most gracious."

"And as always, you are being most diplomatic.

But you were not quite ready to be rescued, I see that now. I am sorry, Cathy . . . Michael. I could call back—"

"Oh, the papers would have a field day with that one," Michael said.

Miserable as she felt, Cathy had to laugh. "I can see the headlines: *Missing Millionaire Chooses to Stay Lost.*"

"That would be the truth if I *had* a choice; you know that, don't you Cathy?"

And because she loved him, she took it as truth, and nodded.

"If you'll excuse me, I'll just check on dessert." Marrisa got up, the faint slap of her sandals on tile following her into the kitchen.

Michael walked around the table and opened his arms to Cathy. She slipped inside their warm, familiar circle. "I love you," he said into her hair.

"I love you too,' she answered, tipping her head back.

"Then there's no problem."

"None." She tightened her arms around his waist.

"You guarantee that, right?" he asked, half laughingly, his eyes suddenly strangely vulnerable. "I didn't expect this to be happening so fast."

"Leave it to you to know the only princess with the only phone within a hundred miles, Mr. Winters." She shook her curly head, teasing him.

"If I'd known, I would have headed for a different island. One with just a telegraph. Two cans strung on a line."

"Tom-toms." She grinned back, and then her brows swooped low. "Oh, Michael, I was good at tossing matches into the ocean, but what do I know about sabotaging phones . . . or helicopters?"

"Think you could take an emergency course?"

"Yes." She smiled through her tears.

He held her face between his hands and kissed her gently on the mouth.

"You call that a kiss?" she demanded, and kissed him back, hard.

From outside came the sound of birds crying in the distance, their sharp, startled calls filling the bright sunlight. And then they heard the whir of the helicopter's blades.

The sound shattered the silence like pieces of broken crystal, and Cathy felt her optimism shatter along with it.

"Oh, Michael—" she cried, but Marissa swept in, Jessa on her heels, and suddenly the whole room was filled with commotion.

"They're here," the princess announced.

Fourteen

It was a short trip, unbelievably short. The wide blue ocean it would have taken days to sail across, they flew over in only an hour: a miracle of modern technology.

Cathy wanted those days, those hours and minutes and seconds.

In the helicopter there was the pilot, the accountant who had to fill Michael in on a million details, the chatter of the princess, the whir of the blades. Cathy sat in the backseat, pretending to look at a magazine. She felt utterly and completely lost. Every few minutes Michael would turn in his seat, crane his neck, look back at her, and smile. Cathy waved her fingers and smiled back reassuringly. But her heart was breaking.

"Here we are, Mr. Winters," the pilot said. "Right on schedule, and you've got yourself a welcoming committee."

Michael groaned. Cathy could feel it, and she had to smile, thinking of how fiercely he'd be frowning; she knew what he was feeling: his annoyance, his irritation. He was thinking of their wide sandy beach, and the lobsters waiting to be caught, and the trade wind blowing, and he'd be pushing that all aside into a separate compartment, getting ready to deal with reporters and photographers, impatient with the whole thing before it even happened, pulling on his armor, gearing up. . . .

He turned back to her. "Can you believe this?" he grumbled across the rows, his eyes locking into hers, wanting what they were leaving, needing her.

"It'll be okay." She waved it all away. "Give 'em a couple of pictures and a few heroic words and they'll be happy. If they bother you too much, I'll just have a sudden relapse of some dread tropical fever and keep them busy till you can get away."

"Thanks, pal." He smiled.

"You're welcome, pal."

He reached back through the space between the seats and she took his hand, twining her fingers with his, holding tight for a second until the helicopter settled and the door was shoved open.

"Mr. Winters! Mr. Winters! Is it true you were shipwrecked? . . . Where have you been? . . . Have you heard about the merger between MorTech and Metro Development? . . . Were you alone all this time? . . . Are you going to give up any of the property that Wintex now holds in the mid-Atlantic region?"

The flashbulbs exploded as he stepped out. He looked handsomer than ever with his shirt open at the collar, his sleeves rolled up to the elbow. He was tan, fit, and rugged. The scene was absolutely guaranteed to sell another hundred million magazines.

Someone shoved a microphone in his face. Michael swallowed a sharp retort, forced a smile, and said, "It was a hell of an adventure, and I'll have a press statement for you all in an hour. Thanks for showing up. And now we've got to get to our rooms and clean up. Thanks." With at quick glance over his shoulder to make sure Cathy was okay, he strode on up to the hotel.

A reporter, a fellow with keen eyes and a good nose for news, put his hand on Cathy's arm. "I recognize Princess Marissa and the others, but I haven't met you before. Ms.?" His words lifted into a question that expected an answer.

"Stephenson," Cathy replied softly.

"And—?"

"And I'd better get going."

"Going where? And where have you been? You look very tan and healthy, as if you've been outdoors a great deal lately."

Cathy tilted her head to the side. "Funny how deceptive appearances can be. I actually have this terrible tropical fever, and I can just feel my temperature climbing."

"I bet your temperature's been climbing," the man said, eyeing Cathy with a knowing smile. "Well, I hope we'll have a chance to talk another time."

"That would be nice." Cathy nodded, and followed the others into the hotel.

Her room was on the floor below Michael's. She had nothing to put in the drawers or hang in the closets, so she sat down on the edge of the bed. Such a big bed, with a white lace comforter and two pillows. It made her sad. For the first time in many nights, she wouldn't pillow her head on Michael's shoulder, wouldn't sleep with her hand thrown across his chest, wouldn't wake to see his dark head there next to hers.

She started crying and couldn't stop. It was silly. Nothing had changed really, nothing had been decided, but she felt washed with grief, aching, alone, as if someone had died.

"Stop it!" she commanded herself, and wiped her face with the back of her hand, but the tears wouldn't stop. It was awful, stupid, and embarrassing.

Grabbing a tissue, she placed a phone call through to the States. The phone rang in Indiana, and her grandmother picked it up. "Hello?"

"Gap? Hi, it's me, it's Cathy."

"Well, of course I know who 'me' is! How are you, dear?"

"I'm fine. I'm fine, Gap. I'm calling from some islands over near the Bahamas."

"The Bahamas? Oh, my, Cathy—"

"I hope you haven't been worried, I haven't been able to get to a phone until now, but everything's okay."

"No, no, I wasn't worried, dear. I knew in my bones that you were all right. I figured you were out having that adventure we talked about—"

"I was, Gap. I mean, I *am;* it's not over." *Oh, please don't let it be over.*

"That's wonderful," her grandmother said. She paused, and then filled in the empty space. "So . . .

is that all the news I'm going to get from the Bahamas for now?"

"For now." Cathy laughed. "But I'll report back with an update, don't worry."

She heard her grandmother's affectionate chuckle. "I'll stay tuned!"

"Okay. Hugs to Aunt Tisha. I love you."

"Love you too, girl."

There. She was still Cathy Stephenson. Still the same whole, capable woman. Michael still loved her. Everything was fine. Right?

A knock at the door sent her leaping across the room. She yanked the door open, then stepped back in surprise. It was the accountant.

"Mr. Winters asked me to deliver these," he said, holding out a huge stack of boxes. "There is a note on top."

"Thanks." Cathy took the packages in her arms. "Thanks a lot."

She shut the door with one foot, then tumbled the pile across the bed as she searched for the note.

Dearest Cathy,

I love you. It's mayhem up here, and I don't know when I can get away. If you're starving, go on to dinner without me. But if you can wait, I'll call the minute I can get away. I love you. Oh, told you that, but I guess twice can't hurt.

Michael

The last line had been scrawled in a careless hand, and she could almost hear his husky laughter, see the grin lifting to his blue eyes. She knew the shade, the exact shade his eyes were when he laughed. She always would.

When the phone did ring hours later, it woke her out of a troubled sleep.

"Michael?" she murmured, forgetting to be cautious.

"Yes," he said softly. "Did I wake you?"

"I guess so. Yes, I—I was waiting, but . . ." Her words were lost in a yawn.

He gave a low chuckle, sounding tired himself. "It's after midnight. I'm sorry. I couldn't get away till now. Are you up for a late dinner? Or maybe you'd rather go back to sleep—"

"No! I'm wide awake, honest. And starving. Do you want to meet downstairs or—"

"I'll come knock on your door. Ten minutes?"

"Less!"

She was ready, dressed in white linen slacks and a silk blouse—bra, panties, shoes, bag, the whole works—when he knocked.

She pulled the odor open, and felt a thrill of joy run through her. "Hi, Michael!"

Michael stepped inside, pushed the door closed, and took her in his arms. "Oh, Cathy, how I've missed you."

"I know," she whispered, wrapping her arms around his waist and lifting her cheek to his. "Oh" —she laughed, her eyes shining—"you feel strange without your beard. And dressed in a pinstriped shirt"—she pulled back to see him more fully—"and a suit, oh, my!"

"Back to the old Michael Winters." He grinned, and pulled her back close to him. *The old Michael Winters*, Cathy repeated to herself. She could feel the tension in his arms, across his back under the expensive jacket. Even as he held her he felt coiled like a spring—tight and tense.

"Culture shock," she whispered to him, her eyes carefully watching his face.

"You bet. It's back to the real world with a vengeance." His mouth settled into a straight, hard line. Then he released her and rubbed at the back of his neck, rolling his shoulders. He smiled down at her. "Well, I certainly kept you waiting for dinner. Shall we go?"

"Why don't we stay?" Cathy slid her hand down his arm until she held his hand. She took a step toward the bed.

Something close to pain flashed behind Michael's eyes. "I've got to put a call in to L.A. at two A.M. And a six-o'clock wake-up call for a seven o'clock meeting. It wouldn't work, Cathy."

"Sure it would. I don't want to sleep now anyway, and I can leave a wake-up call here too—"

"And who would answer in *my* room?"

"You could be in the shower—"

"You'll be exhausted."

"I don't care!"

"It doesn't make any sense, Cathy."

"Since when have we had to make sense?"

"I've *always* had to make sense." He cut her off with the sharpness of his words. And then he turned away, shoving his hands into his pockets. His back looked like a wide, hard wall.

His eyes would be that slate gray, dark as thunderstorms. And that frown line would be there again, between his dark brows. And the corner of his mouth would be turned down, pulling at the left side of his face in that harsh look of impatience. She didn't even have to see it, she knew it. She knew him. Dammit, she knew him and she loved him!

"Michael, I vote for bed."

He turned and grinned at her. "You can take your hands off your hips, Indiana. Tonight you're overruled. Hey—" He stepped close and rested his chin on the top of her head. "I'm really beat. I need some dinner, and a glass of wine, and just a friend for company tonight, okay?"

She shook her head, her lower lip caught between her teeth. "I don't think you know what you really need, Michael, but if that's what you want—"

"Thanks, Cathy."

"You're welcome." She sighed and followed him out the door.

They sat down for dinner in a little corner of the nearly empty restaurant.

"We kept the kitchen open for you, Mr. Winters," the waiter said.

"Thank you. And thank the manager for me. Tell her I really appreciate it."

"No problem, sir."

Cathy shook her head, her brows lifting into her curly bangs. "I forgot what it was like to be with you when you're Michael Winters, Wheeler-Dealer."

"So did I," he said softly. "By the way, how did you like the clothes?"

"Oh, the clothes, they were wonderful. *Are* wonderful," she corrected herself, running her hands over the silk of her blouse. "But you didn't have to do that, Michael."

"I wanted to. I thought it was the least I could do, considering you started out fully dressed somewhere at the beginning of all this."

Their eyes met, and he gave her a lopsided grin, then looked down at his menu.

"So, what would you like, Cathy?"

"You."

"Cathy—" he warned.

"You asked." She shrugged, tipped her head, and offered a smile. "You want me to play nice, Michael? You want me to just be polite? Okay, I'll have a shrimp cocktail and a salad. That's what I'd like."

"I just want to keep everything under control, everything easy—"

"Oh, Michael!" She gave a startled little laugh. "I don't think that should be what we want. We can want *more* than that. Easy or not, I'd vote for a little chaos if there's love involved."

"What you don't understand is that there's a lot involved here in this other world I live in. There are things you don't know anything about. An empire. A whole world!"

"You're my whole world, Michael, that's all I know."

Instead of the smile, the touch she expected, her words evoked a stiff silence. She stared at him a moment, then dropped her eyes, feeling absolutely naked in all her new clothes.

• • •

When they met downstairs the next day at noon by accident, she actually felt awkward.

"Morning, Michael." She smiled, not sure whether to hug him, touch him, or turn tail and flee. "So, how's everything?"

"Wild. The merger on the West Coast really shook up the market. I've got a stack of Faxes this high—" He measured with his palms and she saw how rough his hands still were, weatherbeaten, sunburned, the fingertips callused and blunt—

"Cathy?"

"Oh, I'm sorry, I wasn't listening."

"What were you thinking about?"

She looked up at him. "Lobsters. Fishing. Mussels on the beach."

"Cathy—" He shook his head, his eyes gone slate dark.

"So, do you need some help with the correspondence?" she asked, chin tipped up, her eyes holding his. "Is there *anything* I can do, Michael?"

"I don't think so," he said softly.

She nodded.

Although she hated herself, she had to drop her eyes so he wouldn't see her tears. She set her mouth, gave a sharp little sigh. "Well, I guess I'll go roam around for a while."

"Cathy?" He stopped her with a word. "Meet me for dinner? About eight? Would you?"

She turned back to him. "Maybe. I'll try. But I really do think I've got a touch of some kind of fever. Nothing to worry about," she added quickly, "but I may need to just sleep it off." She turned and hurried back upstairs.

• • •

But she could not resist him. Walking into the bar at seven, she spotted Michael immediately. He was talking to the accountant and another man in a dark business suit, his whole body tight with strain, punctuating his words with sharp, incisive gestures. When the accountant spoke, Michael reached up and rubbed the back of his neck. She could feel his weariness.

And somehow he could feel her presence.

In mid-sentence he turned, searched the room for her, and waved her over.

"Hi, Cathy, how are you?" he asked, slipping an arm around her waist.

"I'm fine, Michael. But you look exhausted."

"It's been one of those days." He laughed. Then he drew a deep breath. "Well, why don't we call it *caput* for today, gentlemen? Roger, let me know if you hear anything from London, otherwise I'm done for tonight. See you both tomorrow. And thanks."

"Night, Michael."

"Good night, Mr. Winters."

And then they were alone.

"Whew . . ." He rolled his head around, trying to loosen the muscles knotted across his shoulders. "One helluva day."

"Does it have to be, Michael? Can't you just . . . I don't know, just *do* less?"

"I don't know how to do that, Cathy," he answered honestly, looking deep into her eyes. Then he smiled. "Maybe you'll have to fall into the sea again, so I can rescue you, and we can start all over."

She touched his cheek. "Sounds a bit drastic to me, Mr. Winters."

He laughed, rubbing his forehead with one hand. "Guess so, Indiana. But it sure sounds tempting."

She caught his hand in hers, then the other, pushing her fingers between his until they were connected, hands, arms, bodies, and she could feel his blood pulsing. "Let's try it, Michael. Some midway point that will work, a compromise, something halfway between fairy tales and this. Some way to be both Michael Winters—"

He tightened his fingers around hers. "How? Tell me how to do it, Cathy. I want to—oh, God, I want to! But I don't think it would work."

"Give it a shot!"

He laughed. "You know me, I take only calculated risks."

"No, you don't! You dive for lobsters! You climb coconut trees! You sail over reefs, Papa!"

"That's in fantasies."

"No, it isn't. It's just a different reality. We can mix the two. I know we can!"

"You think so, huh?" He grinned down at her.

"Yes!" she answered with all her Indiana certainty.

"Oh, Mr. Winters, excuse me—"

It was the accountant, back again and red-faced. "It's London. There was a fax waiting when I got upstairs. They're ready to sign, and they've got our contact in Lucerne committed as well. They want a meeting, tomorrow. Four P.M. I've got the jet fueling and we'll need to leave in the morning."

"In the morning?" Michael and Cathy spoke at once, their words colliding in midair.

Cathy looked down, blinking madly to keep the tears from spilling. Do something, Michael. *Say something. Don't let this happen*, she thought wildly.

"Then you'll have to book Ms. Stephenson on an early flight to Orlando. Take care of that now, would you please, Roger?"

It hurt to draw breath. Cathy had to hunch her shoulders together, waiting for the pain to ease.

"Cathy, maybe it'll work out best this way. There's just no time to deal with anything now. You can get back to Orlando and I'll tie this all up in Europe, and then I'll come back and we'll get together—"

"Are you crazy?" She pressed her hand to her mouth as if to catch the words. But it was too late.

"I'm sorry," she said quickly. "I guess you're right. I . . . I . . ." she stuttered, shrugged in despair, having no idea of the right way to do this impossible thing. "You must be right. I do have so much to do. I need to look for a job. And you're so busy—"

"But I'll be back soon. I'll call the minute I get back to the States. I can fly you up and we'll have time to talk, and think about the future and—"

"—what? Evaluate our options?" She shook her head, numbed with grief. But high in her chest the pain began to flutter. Another minute, and she didn't know if she could stand it. "Michael, I love you. But right now you have to excuse me. I'm going upstairs, right now—"

"Wait, Cathy!" Michael grabbed her arm, and for one fleeting second she thought he might say the right words, make it all better, close the horrible widening gulf between them . . . and keep her world from falling apart. She looked up at him, her love shining in her eyes, holding her breath.

But he squared his jaw and shoved both hands into his pockets as if *he* had some reason to be angry. "I've *got* to get everything under control, Cathy. This is the real world, not some damn fairy tale!"

Left with nothing but a little pride, she did not answer.

Fifteen

How could a fairy tale hurt so much? How could it cause such sadness and pain? Especially when she'd known it was a dream all along.

And if all those days had been just some fantasy, then why was she sitting here on Delta 161 to Orlando crying real tears into a crumpled tissue?

Oh, take off already! Cathy cried silently. She couldn't stand the sight of the palm trees, the curve of blue water, the smooth pink sand that reached almost to the runway. Almost. Almost did not count for anything, that was one thing she knew for sure.

There was the word *almost* spoken. There was the touch *almost* shared. There was the dream that *almost* came true. And then there was nothing.

Nothing but pain. And the sharpest pain of all was the sight of him standing back at the gate, one hand raised in farewell. How could he say good-bye to her? She couldn't say it to him. She had run aboard without looking back at him, and she couldn't bear to look at him now. She ducked her head into her shredded tissue and wept.

Michael had tried to follow her silhouette on board, had tried to count the windows back and guess where she'd be sitting. But he couldn't see her from where he was. He'd lost sight of her. He felt it like a wound, like the loss of an arm or a leg, like some gaping hole where his heart had been. The sweat was running down under his arms, across his chest. When the engines raced to life, he felt the pain rise to his throat, threatening to choke him.

Cathy! The sound roared through his head. He wanted to yell, hit something, break down the damn gate and run after her. So why didn't he?

There was the meeting in London. The jet already fueled. Millions on the line.

Cathy's plane began to roll down the runway.

He started moving along the fence, keeping his eyes on the window that might be hers, waving, not knowing he was running until he ran into a man who reeled back with a sharp, angry look. "Watch where you goin', mon!"

"Sorry!" Michael hardly felt the jolt. He just ran on, his eyes locked on the plane as if the strength of his gaze would bind it, stop it on the runway. He hit the end of the fence. There was no place to go.

Cathy!

The plane rose, taking her with it. Cathy. Everything he wanted, everything he needed, everything he loved in this world.

The minute she was out of reach, he knew she was the center of his life. Everything else would have to fit around her. Because without her, none of it was worth a damn. Without her, there was nothing.

He ran back up to the gate area, arms pumping in his suit jacket.

His accountant and his chief mechanic had been watching his unexpected behavior from a distance, and now they stood there openmouthed, waiting to see what was going to happen next.

"Plane ready?" Michael shouted as he neared them.

"Yes, sir!"

"Great. Put a fax through to the sheikh—here, take this down, Roger, word for word. And hurry. And then wire London—the meeting's on hold till I get back."

"Till you get *back*, sir? From where? When?"

"Tell you the truth, I don't know when," he said, breathing hard. And then he grinned. "As soon as I marry that girl."

Fifteen minutes later his private jet took off, climbed to 27,000 feet, and raced off after Delta 161.

If Cathy had known to look out the window, she would have seen the small gleaming plane tucked beneath her big white one there in the clear, bright Caribbean skies. But she was too busy crying. And after a while the small jet pulled ahead, determined to beat her to Orlando.

When Cathy landed, she followed the crowd in its still-on-vacation mood, one sad little island in a rush of noise and merrymaking. The others had piles of suitcases, cases of liquor, shopping bags full of per-

ume and watches, gold jewelry, and fine crystal.
Cathy had empty hands and a heart that matched.

"Nothing to declare, miss?" the customs agent
asked, eyeing her suspiciously.

"No," she whispered, head down and sniffing.

"Are you sure? Haven't you brought anything back
with you?"

"No!" She lifted her head and met his eyes with
surprising vehemence. "I left it all behind. And it
isn't my fault. I *know* what's real, and I *fought* for
it! It just didn't do any good."

The agent looked baffled. Did she mean porcelain,
crystal, gold? Should he ask? Poor girl, she looked
so lovely but so sad. Maybe she'd been robbed. She
didn't have a passport: just temporary identifica-
tion. "Now, miss," he offered consolingly, "it can't be
that bad—"

"It's worse than that," she cried. "I lost everything
that matters."

"Do you want to file a claim?"

Cathy shook her head and slipped away, the tears
balancing on the ends of her lashes.

She had to get out of there before she really made
a fool of herself. She looked around for a sign for
taxis or buses, some means of escape. There were all
kinds of people holding signs: signs for corporate
connections, tour groups, prearranged transportation. Her eyes swam over them all blindly, then flew
back with a start to one man, a handsome man in a
suit and a pale blue button-down shirt that matched
his eyes. Michael. Michael Winters, the Great American Bachelor. And he was holding a sign.

Cathy could not breathe. And the floor was tilting

beneath her feet. It couldn't be him. She'd just spent two lovely weeks lost in a fairy tale, dreaming an impossible dream, and now her heart was playing tricks on her. Cathy squeezed her eyes shut tight. But trick or not, she would risk anything to see him one more time . . . even the pain of having him vanish. So she opened her eyes and looked again.

Oh!

Dreams didn't stop hearts. Michael did. Fairy tales didn't hurt. They came true.

Cautiously, she edged forward through the crowds of people, her eyes never leaving his face until she could see for sure that he was smiling, grinning that heart-stopping grin at her, his eyes shining. And then she looked up at the sign he held.

It read: MARRY ME.

Cathy's heart fluttered to her throat. She bit her lips and came as close as she could, leaning over the rope. "What about London? What about business?" she whispered.

"I can do it all. With you I can do anything, or nothing, whatever we want, whatever we decide together."

"You're sure, Michael?" she asked, watching his eyes.

"I love you, Cathy."

"Those are the magic words." She nodded, letting her smile climb from her lips to her soft brown eyes. "And I love you too."

She held her hand out and pulled him through the gate, against traffic. "Come with me!" She held his hand tight and led him back to customs.

"It's me again. I *do* have something to declare,"

she announced to the same startled agent. "A friend . . . a husband."

"How nice." The man laughed.

"And an island," Michael added, pulling Cathy close. "I bought back Yellowtail Cay for a wedding gift, from me to you. I want to see you there, with Gap and your aunt rocking on the front porch. And we can have a cat."

The agent laughed. "Are you declaring *all* those? There's a special form for a cat."

"The only form we need now," Michael whispered softly into her hair, "is a marriage license."

"That means we know the ending to this story." Cathy tipped up her chin and smiled deep into his eyes.

"And they lived happily ever after."

THE EDITOR'S CORNER

This month we're inaugurating a special and permanent feature that is dear to our hearts. From now on we'll spotlight one Fan of the Month at the end of the Editor's Corner. Through the years we've enjoyed and profited from your praise, your criticisms, your analyses. So have our authors. We want to share the joy of getting to know a devoted romance reader with all of you other devoted romance readers—thus, this feature. We hope you'll enjoy getting to know our first Fan of the Month, Pat Diehl.

Our space is limited this month due to the addition of our new feature, so we can give you only a few tasty tidbits about each upcoming book.

Leading off is Kay Hooper with LOVESWEPT #360, **THE GLASS SHOE,** the second in her *Once Upon a Time* series. This modern Cinderella story tells the tale of beautiful heiress Amanda Wilderman and dashing entrepreneur Ryder Foxx, who meet at a masquerade ball. Their magical romance will enchant you, and the fantasy never ends—not even when the clock strikes midnight!

Gail Douglas is back with *The Dreamweavers*: **GAMBLING LADY,** LOVESWEPT #361, also the second in a series. Captaining her Mississippi riverboat keeps Stefanie Sinclair busy, but memories of her whirlwind marriage to Cajun rogue T.J. Carriere haunt her. T.J. never understood what drove them apart after only six months, but he vows to win his wife back. Stefanie doesn't stand a chance of resisting T.J.—and neither will you!

LOVESWEPT #362, **BACK TO THE BEDROOM** by Janet Evanovich, will have you in stitches! For months David Dodd wanted to meet the mysterious woman who was always draped in a black cloak and carrying a large, odd case—and he finally gets the chance when a helicopter drops a chunk of metal through his lovely neighbor's roof and he rushes to her rescue. Katherine Finn falls head over heels for David, but as a dedicated concert musician, she can't fathom the man who seems to be drifting through life. This wonderful story is sure to strike a chord with you!

Author Fran Baker returns with another memorable romance, **KING OF THE MOUNTAIN,** LOVESWEPT #363. Fran deals with a serious subject in **KING OF THE MOUNTAIN,** and she handles it beautifully. Heroine Kitty

• *(continued)*

Reardon carries deep emotional scars from a marriage to a man who abused her, and hero Ben Cooper wants to offer her sanctuary in his arms. But Kitty is afraid to reach out to him, to let him heal her soul. This tenderly written love story is one you won't soon forget.

Iris Johansen needs no introduction, and the title of her next LOVESWEPT, #364, **WICKED JAKE DARCY,** speaks for itself. But we're going to tantalize you anyway! Mary Harland thinks she's too innocent to enchant the notorious rake Jake Darcy, but she's literally swept off her feet by the man who is temptation in the flesh. Dangerous forces are at work, however, forcing Mary to betray Jake and begin a desperate quest. We bet your hearts are already beating in double-time in anticipation of this exciting story. Don't miss it!

From all your cards and letters, we know you all just love a bad-boy hero, and has Charlotte Hughes got one for you in **SCOUNDREL,** LOVESWEPT #365. Growing up in Peculiar, Mississippi, Blue Mitchum had been every mother's nightmare, and every daughter's fantasy. When Cassie Kennard returns to town as Cassandra D'Clair, former world-famous model, she never expects to encounter Blue Mitchum again—and certainly never guessed he'd be mayor of the town! Divorced, the mother of twin girls, Cassie wants to start a new life where she feels safe and at home, but Blue's kisses send her into a tailspin! These two people create enough heat to singe the pages. Maybe we should publish this book with a warning on its cover!

Enjoy next month's LOVESWEPTs and don't forget to keep in touch!

Sincerely,

Carolyn Nichols

Carolyn Nichols
Editor
LOVESWEPT
Bantam Books
666 Fifth Avenue
New York, NY 10103